D0382102

DOCTOR · WHO

# The Stealers
# of Dreams

DOCTOR·WHO

# The Stealers of Dreams

## BY STEVE LYONS

BBC
BOOKS

Published by BBC Books, BBC Worldwide Ltd,
Woodlands, 80 Wood Lane, London W12 0TT

First published 2005

ISBN 0 563 48638 4

Commissioning Editors: Shirley Patton/Stuart Cooper
Creative Director & Editor: Justin Richards

Doctor Who is a BBC Wales production for BBC ONE
Executive Producers: Russell T Davies, Julie Gardner and Mal Young
Producer: Phil Collinson

This book is a work of fiction. Names, characters, places and
incidents are either a product of the author's imagination or
used fictitiously. Any resemblance to actual people living
or dead, events or locales is entirely coincidental.

Cover design by Henry Steadman © BBC 2005
Typeset in Albertina by Rocket Editorial, Aylesbury, Bucks
Printed and bound in Germany by GGP Media GmbH

For more information about this and other BBC books,
please visit our website at www.bbcshop.com

*For the Monday Night Group*
*– Dave, John, Pete, Phil and Tracy –*
*for having the imagination…*

It was there again, at the foot of the bed. She could hear it.

She tried to do as she had been told. She gritted her teeth and closed her eyes and made a humming sound in the back of her throat to block out its shuffling and its scraping. She tried to focus on that, and on the drone of the night-time traffic far below.

It worked, for a short time. The noise was cathartic; it made her feel brave. Until she ran out of breath.

Then she lay shivering in the darkness, hot on the outside but cold on the inside, face buried in her pillow and sheets wrapped around her as if she could hide from it.

As if it might go away.

Kimmi didn't want to be a bad girl. But the monster was real. It was real and it wouldn't leave her alone.

'An overactive imagination,' the doctors at the Big White House had said.

'You're fifteen years old, Kimmi,' her mother had sobbed, tearing at her bedraggled hair. 'You can't live in this... this fantasy world any longer. It's dangerous, don't you see? You have to grow up. Why can't you... why can't you be like all the other kids? Why can't you be normal?'

Kimmi hated seeing her mother like that. That was why she had kept it from her for so long.

That, and the incident at school two years ago. It had been her first week. Her teacher had snatched the data pad from her desk, seen the open file and let out a scandalised gasp. Kimmi hadn't thought much of it before then; she had just been daydreaming, letting her hands wander.

No one had cared about her doodles at junior school. She couldn't understand why they were all making such a fuss now; why the eyes of her classmates burned into her, some shocked, some mocking, some feeling her embarrassment.

'Perhaps you can explain to me,' the teacher had said in tones dripping with contempt, 'what this diagram has to do with the life-support requirements of the early space pioneers. What it has to do with anything real. I've certainly never seen such a grotesque creature in real life. Have you? Have any of you?'

'The product of a diseased mind,' the email home had said.

In the Big White House, they had shown Kimmi shapes on a computer. They had asked her what they were, then told her she was wrong.

She had tried to argue at first, tried to tell them about the monster, but she didn't like the taste of the pills they gave her, so she had learned to agree with them. She agreed that the shapes were just shapes and that the monster wasn't real.

And she had drawn in secret after that. Until today. Until this afternoon, when Mum had arrived home early and surprised her.

She had snatched her pad away just like the teacher had, dashed it to the floor. She had shaken Kimmi until her bones had rattled. She had cried a lot.

Kimmi had cried too, sent to bed without supper, hysterical threats ringing in her ears. 'Do you want to have to go back to that place again? *Do you?*'

She had dozed, for a time, and woken in the dark. With the monster.

She was listening for it, though she didn't want to hear it. She couldn't help it. Her senses were hyper-alert.

There was nothing. She ought to have been relieved. But what if the monster was just doing as she was: staying very still and very quiet, trying to trick her?

She had no choice. She had to look. She raised her head hesitantly, praying under her breath until she remembered what the doctors had told her about prayer.

She stared for a long time, trying to make sense of the shadows. They were moving, twisting, but that was just because of the info-screen on the building across the road, casting its light patterns through the gap in her curtains. Wasn't it?

Then, a moment's white light and she saw it. Its muscular black shape, hunched into a crouch, a wizened limb draped lazily over the seat of her chair.

Or was it just the shape of her own clothing, cast aside in resentment?

She was paralysed, her throat dry. She wanted to yell, but she knew what would happen if she did. Mum would come and she would turn on the light and the monster would be gone, and she would be upset again.

What if she turned on the light herself? What if she could will herself to cross that expanse of carpet, to reach for the sensor?

And what if the monster leaped on her from behind and clawed her down?

They'd know she wasn't lying then. Too late.

She was a big girl now. That was what Mum had said. Big enough to be logical about this. If the monster was real, then why hadn't it killed her already?

The doctors had asked her that question. She had

answered that maybe it was because she had always kept as still as she could. They had glanced at one another, shaking their heads.

'We're just trying to help you. Do you want to be frightened all your life?' they had said.

And Kimmi decided now, lying in the dark, paralysed by the presence of the monster, that she didn't want that at all. She would find the strength. She would stand and walk to the light sensor. She would activate it, and she would turn and look. Towards the foot of the bed. At the monster.

Then she would know, one way or another.

She thought she heard a warning hiss as her first foot touched the floor. She thought the monster had tensed, readying itself to pounce. And she was frozen again, one foot in the bed and one out.

She heard its breathing, but it might have been her own breath loud in her ears. She caught the glint of its eye, but it might have been a flicker from the info-screen outside reflecting off the smaller screen in here.

She heard it growl, and this time she was suddenly, terrifyingly sure.

Kimmi leaped out of bed as the monster sprang for her. She felt it brush against the back of her nightdress, and the impact as it thudded into the mattress behind her. It roared, and she screamed as she leaped for the sensor, desperately praying that she'd reach it in time, that the light would work.

Then the monster was upon her. She could feel its hot breath, flecked with spittle, on her neck, and its claws in her shoulders and ribs. She could feel its thick tail binding her legs, tripping her. She fell, and its weight bore her down. She was wailing and kicking and hammering her fists into the carpet impotently.

And somehow she managed to dislodge the monster from her back, managed to roll over and, for a heady instant, thought she could escape it.

But then its great black mass was rearing over her again, and its claws stabbed through her shoulders and pinned her to the floor. And all Kimmi could see was its big black mouth, with its triple rows of teeth.

And little tufts of blue hair sprouting from the monster's bottom lip.

Just like in her pictures.

# ONE

**C**hips had been a mistake. Rose blamed the Doctor. He was used to this travelling lark. Other worlds, other times. He ought to have tipped her the wink, explained to her that chips here weren't chipped potatoes but chipped something-or-other-else. Some local vegetable, a bit too soft, a bit too blue, with an oily texture and a peppery aftertaste.

As she pushed her plate aside, though, she felt a familiar tingle. Sometimes it took just that sort of incidental detail to remind her how far she was from home; that she was breathing the air of the future. The air of another world.

*Another world…*

Rose still found it hard to take in, as if it was too much for her mind to process all at once and it would only let her focus on one thing at a time. It didn't help that this particular world was so human, so…

*mundane.* Crowded pavements littered with discarded wrappers, streets clogged with traffic, and the buildings... Almost without exception, they were concrete towers, devoid of character, no more than boxes to hold people. Like the ones on the estate back home, thought Rose, built before she was born. How disappointing!

It could almost have been London, or any big American city. Peering through the grease-streaked window beside their table, she eyed a line of cars simmering resentfully at a nearby junction. She would hardly have been surprised to see a big red bus turning that corner.

Look at the details, she thought. Like the menu, no thicker than a normal piece of cardboard and yet it projected life-sized aromagrams of its featured dishes. And the way the cars floated over the roadway on air jets, churning the gravel beneath them. And the TV screens, as flat as posters, seemingly attached to every available surface.

That had been her first impression of this place: newsreaders looking down at her from the sides of every building, their words subtitled so as not to be lost in the ever-present traffic grumble. There were two screens in the café itself, one behind Rose and one on the wall in front. She kept finding her eyes drawn to this second one over Captain Jack's shoulder:

Mr Anton Ryland the Sixth of Sector Four-Four-Kappa-Zero was celebrating today after a well-earned promotion. Mr Ryland, who has worked for the Office of Statistical Processing for thirty-seven years, is now a Senior Analytical Officer, Blue Grade. Commenting on his rapid rise, Mr Ryland said, 'It means I earn an additional 2.4 credits per day before tax, and my parking space –'

The Doctor had been attacking his food with the same gusto with which he tackled Autons and Slitheen and other alien menaces. As he glanced up between forkfuls, though, his eyes followed Rose's gaze and his lips pulled into a grimace. 'Yeah, I know,' he said, 'not exactly "Man Bites Dog", is it? You want those chips?'

'Suits me to have a bit of downtime,' said Jack nonchalantly, biting into his burger – and Rose didn't even want to *think* about what manner of alien creature that might have come from. Those chips had opened up one hell of a mental can of worms.

Jack hadn't known the Doctor for as long as she had, but the lifestyle was nothing new to him. Born in the fifty-first century – allegedly – he claimed to have spent his life in the space lanes, even travelled in time.

Of course, you couldn't always believe a word Jack said.

'Wouldn't wanna live here, though,' he continued

in his American drawl. 'This must be the most boring planet in the universe!'

'Er, do you mind?' said the Doctor. 'I don't do "boring". There's something new and exciting to find on every world if you look for it.'

'Y'know,' Rose teased, 'I thought it was only in naff old films that people in the future wore those one-piece jumpsuits.'

'Yeah, I figure that's why they've been giving us the eye,' said Jack. 'Our gear.'

The Doctor frowned. 'They have?'

'A few of them, discreetly. They must think we're pretty eccentric.'

'A while since I've been called that,' said the Doctor.

'Hey, maybe there's a few credits to be made here. What do you say, Rose? Start this world's first fashion house. You design 'em, I flog 'em.'

'This is Rose's future,' the Doctor reminded Jack. 'I doubt she could show these people anything they haven't seen before, at some point in their history.'

'So the car-mechanic look is what?' said Rose. 'A fashion statement?'

'I'm more bothered about the time,' said the Doctor. 'I make it just gone –' he did his usual joke of glancing at his wristwatch – at least, Rose assumed it was a joke – '2775, but the technology here's still stuck in the twenty-seventh century. Earlier.' He sniffed the air thoughtfully.

'And?' Jack prompted.

'And that usually means trouble,' said Rose, relishing a chance to show off her experience. 'It means someone or something is holding back progress, right, Doctor?'

'Maybe. Don't you think it's odd? That these people escaped Earth, found their brave new world, and all they've done is copy what they left behind?' He gave her no time to answer. 'How long do you think this city has been here? Long enough for the dirt to be ground in. Long enough to be bursting at the seams. But what have these people – what have any of them – done about it?'

He raised his voice as he went on, as if personally accusing everyone at the neighbouring tables. Rose leaned forward and spoke quietly, hoping to regain some measure of privacy. 'They *are* building, though. We saw builders on the way in. Remember, they used those floating-disc things instead of scaffolding.'

'On car parks and squares.' The Doctor waved a dismissive hand. 'And I doubt there's a blade of grass left in this city.'

'He's right,' said Jack. 'They're bulldozing skyscrapers to replace them with bigger ones. Building upwards, not outwards. How much of this world did the TARDIS say was jungle, Doctor?'

'Over 90 per cent of its landmass – but we saw no sign of construction at the edge of the city as we came in.'

'The settlers must have cleared an area when they got here.'

'But they haven't expanded since then,' realised Rose. 'They're just… just trying to squeeze more people into the same space.'

'I think it's time we found out a few things about this place. Its name, for a start.' The Doctor twisted in his seat and spotted a middle-aged woman leaving the table behind him. She had just swiped a plastic card through some sort of a reader, and was fumbling to replace it in her hip pouch as she headed for the door. 'You look as if you could settle a bet for us,' he said. 'This planet, what's it called?'

Rose made a show of wincing and covering her eyes. Jack just grinned.

The woman was flustered. 'What is this? You trying to trick me?' She looked around suspiciously, as if expecting to see a camera.

Peering between her fingers, Rose saw the disapproving looks and despairing headshakes of the café's other customers.

'This is Colony World 4378976.Delta-Four,' said the woman. 'I know it by no other name and I'm sure I don't know what you're suggesting. Good day to you!' She barged past the Doctor and bustled out onto the street without a backward glance.

'You see?' said the Doctor triumphantly. 'Scratch the surface and there's usually something going on underneath. Fantastic!' He seized a handful of Rose's chips and stuffed them into his mouth. Then, catching her raised-eyebrow stare, he glanced around and mumbled, 'Oh, let them look. We're the most interesting people in this room.'

'You're mental, you are,' laughed Rose.

'Excuse me, gentlemen, lady. I'm afraid I must ask you to leave.'

A man had appeared at the Doctor's elbow. He was short and stocky, his jumpsuit white instead of the usual grey. He held his head at a tilt and looked down his nose at them. 'Your appearance and behaviour are, ah, confusing my other patrons.'

'Confusing them?' The Doctor leaped on the words.

Rose didn't know whether to be angry or amused. 'We weren't disturbing anyone.'

'You mean to say you're kicking us out for dressing a little differently?' said Jack.

'Listen, mate, this is hardly the Savoy!'

'Go now,' said the white-clad man sniffily, 'and I might overlook the fact that you were all heard lying on these premises.'

'It's all right,' said the Doctor quickly, leaping to his feet. 'Time we were off anyway. And you were right about the chips, Rose. They're rubbish.'

The manager cleared his throat meaningfully. 'There is the matter of your bill, sir.'

The Doctor patted down the pockets of his battered

leather jacket, then shared an abashed look with his two friends. Meanwhile, the voice of the television newsreader boomed at them from each side:

> Mrs Helene Flangan is the luckiest woman in Sector One-Beta this evening. Usually, when the 31- year-old schoolteacher drives home from work in her seven-year-old 1.5g injection Mark 14.B family vehicle, the journey takes her an average of forty-two and a half minutes. Tonight, though, she made it in half that time. The reason? Every one of the traffic lights on her route showed green. Earlier, we asked Mrs Flangan what she did with the time she had saved. She spent it watching TV.

There were more flat screens in the foyers of every hotel they visited. When they finally found a room – 'I've just got one on the top floor,' the surly receptionist had grunted. 'The lady'll have to share with you' – there was one in there too, already parading its images before nobody.

Rose flopped onto the single bed and flicked through channels with the remote control, finding news bulletins, news bulletins, news bulletins... something that looked like a drama. Half a dozen twenty-somethings were lounging around on sofas, talking about themselves. 'Reality show,' said the Doctor.

At the café, he'd produced his psychic paper and run it through the card reader on their table. It hadn't worked, of course, but the manager had been easily persuaded that the 'credit card' was real, just a little dog-eared. He'd copied imaginary details onto a data pad, then seen his unwanted customers out.

The paper had done the trick again at the hotel reception. Rose had pointed out that technically this was stealing, but the Doctor had just shrugged. 'Least they can do. I'm about to save their world, probably.'

The receptionist had scooped three small white tablets into a tube and slapped it in front of them with a dour expression. 'To stop you dreaming,' he had said when questioned. The Doctor had tried to refuse, but the receptionist had grunted, 'Up to you whether you take 'em or not, but I gotta provide 'em.'

The room was cramped, its carpet worn and its wallpaper peeling. The bathroom was down the hall somewhere, shared with six more rooms. Rose would rather have slept in the TARDIS, but none of them had fancied another slog through the jungle back to where they had left it. Especially not in the dark. Night had drawn in before they had known it, the ever-present lights of the TV screens fooling their body clocks.

'What from?' asked Jack now. 'You said we're gonna save this world. What from?'

'From its people,' said the Doctor. 'Can't you smell

it? Fossil fuels. They're burning fossil fuels. Not in any great quantities, not yet – but if this society's in regression, as it appears to be…'

'Fossil fuels?' echoed Jack. 'You're yanking my chain.'

'Not about this. It's not right. This wasn't the deal. By the time your race had mastered space travel, you were supposed to have the technology and the maturity not to repeat your mistakes. You've no right to destroy another world!'

There was a long, awkward silence then. For something to do, Rose surfed the TV channels again, filling the air with snatches of information. A man's car had stalled in his garage, making him ten minutes late for work. A teenager had found a one-microcred note in the street and taken it to the police station. A woman had accused her young neighbour of playing unapproved music, but the girl had retaliated with the more serious charge that the complainant was imagining things, and both were now under medical observation.

'What is it with this place?' said Jack. 'It's like they're obsessed with knowing every detail of each other's lives.'

'Nothing wrong with showing an interest,' the Doctor muttered. 'I'm more interested in what we're *not* seeing.'

'It's all news and documentaries,' said Rose.

'They've got, like, thirty TV channels. You'd think I'd have found a soap or something by now.'

'A sitcom,' said the Doctor, 'or a cop show, or one of those hospital dramas you all seem so morbidly fond of.'

'No, hang on.' A new image had appeared: a group of uniformed men and women on a spacious, futuristic set. And it *was* a set; Rose could tell as much without quite knowing how. Something about how it was laid out or lit, the camera angles, or perhaps the way the uniforms delivered their lines so clearly and confidently.

On the screen, a klaxon alarm sounded and the angle changed to show a star field through a curved portal. Two ships dropped into view, all earthy brown and hard angles, though Rose thought they looked a bit too flat to be real.

'They've still got science fiction, then,' she noted.

'Historical reconstruction,' said the Doctor.

Rose shot Jack a withering look, which wiped the smirk from his face.

On the screen, the uniforms had contacted the occupants of the brown craft and were opening trade negotiations. The alarm had been stilled. Boring, thought Rose.

'You can see the pattern, though, can't you?' The Doctor took the remote and zapped through the channels again, hunkering down in front of the screen as if it were the most fascinating thing he'd ever seen. 'News, documentary, news, news, makeover show, news… All factual programmes. There's no escapism. No imagination. Nothing that tells a story.'

'No lies,' realised Jack.

'No fiction.'

Rose couldn't sleep.

It wasn't the unfamiliar surroundings; she was used to that by now. And the blokes had let her have the bed, after she'd vetoed Jack's first suggestion that they all share.

Jack was squashed uncomfortably between the arms of a battered sofa, snoring away, while the Doctor sat in a chair by the window, thinking.

He didn't seem to have moved a muscle in hours. Every so often, Rose looked over and saw him, chin in his arms, his arms resting on the chair back. There was a TV screen outside, playing a light show across his grim-set face. More than once, she thought he must have nodded off until she saw the glint of an alert eye.

The traffic was still heavy down below, the humming of engines and the blare of an occasional frustrated horn acquiring an air of unreality with sixty storeys' distance.

And the Doctor's words were going round in her head…

'OK,' Rose had said with a shrug, 'so they don't like fiction. Does it matter?'

'Of course it matters. Of course it does. Fiction is about possibilities. It's about hopes and dreams and, yeah, fears. Take those things away and what's left? A population of drudges, working, eating, sleeping, watching telly, unable to visualise anything outside the confines of their own dreary lives.'

He had seemed almost personally affronted.

'No wonder this world has stagnated,' he had growled. 'If you can't conceive of something bigger, something better, how can you build it?'

'So what do we do?' Jack had asked, tongue-in-cheek. 'Overthrow the government and introduce story time to the masses?'

'Don't see why not. Do you think it's fair that the people of this world – this human world – have never experienced the works of Charles Dickens?'

'He's a bit of a Dickens nerd,' Rose had confided in an aside to Jack...

Somewhere there were sirens, undulating in tone. A blue light flickered in the window, draining the colours from the screen out there. And if she concentrated hard, she could make out voices, shouting above the traffic.

Rose realised with a start that she had dozed off. She turned to where she had last seen the Doctor, but his chair was empty.

There were footsteps in the corridor outside their door.

Running.

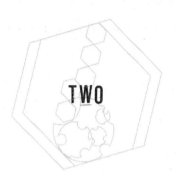

# TWO

The operation had been a shambles. The first police bike to arrive had been shadowed by a camera crew, all lights and sound. The fiction geeks had had a lookout posted – or perhaps they had just been monitoring the live feed on 8 News. They'd been holed up in the cellar of a condemned scraper. One way in, one way out. No one had suggested that they might have prepared an escape route.

A hole in the wall; a tunnel into the sewer pipes. They'd been popping out of personholes all over the sector, running like rats.

For a moment, Inspector Waller was taken by the simile. She pictured the fleeing geeks with whiskers and shrivelled eyes from skulking indoors, hiding from life. Then, feeling that old itch in the back of her brain, she dismissed the thought with an angry shudder.

She had seen the escape on the info-screen at the corner of 34th and 11438th, been halfway there before her vidcom had flared into life. Steel at HQ, with the expected instructions. She had put on her blue lights, but the traffic was packed too densely for the nightshift vehicles to pull out of her way. Fortunately, her police bike was slim enough to weave a path through most of them – and when there was no way around, a brief turbo-charge of the hoverjets would vault her over.

It was as she came down from one such jump, whooping with the adrenaline rush and the butterflies in her stomach, that she found them in her searchlight. Four of them, startled for an instant but recovering quickly and separating, racing for the side streets. The lights of two more bikes blurred by, their riders choosing their targets and shooting after them.

Waller braked hard and came around, finding the tail of the nearest geek.

She lost him for a moment at a corner, rounding it in time to see his back disappearing into a residential building. She smiled to herself, brought the bike up alongside and kicked it into hover mode. She snatched the vidcom from the dashboard and snapped it into its wrist socket, reporting her situation and the last known whereabouts of the fourth runner as she raced for the door.

A nearby screen was tuned to 8 News. The feed had

been pulled, presumably lest it prove too stimulating. A police spokesperson had been wheeled in to give the standard disclaimer, his words subtitled before he had even spoken them:

> *Obviously, this is an unpredictable situation, but I must urge the public to show caution and not to engage in unfounded speculation. The objective facts will be made available in a properly edited form as soon as they are known.*

She was reaching for her override card when she saw that the building's entry panel was broken. So the geek didn't necessarily live here. All the more reason for her not to lose him. Waller shouldered her way into the foyer, checked that the lifts were empty, standing open, and made for the stairs.

He was a flight and a half up. His freckled face appeared over the rail, turning pale at the sight of her. She drew her gun and yelled at him to surrender. He kept running. He was far gone, this one. A rational mind would have accepted the cold fact that escape was impossible.

Waller took the steps at a measured pace, letting the micro-motors in the mesh of her uniform augment her efforts. She could have pushed them harder, but she had no wish to cut the chase short. This was the best part. And she could afford to be patient.

The geek was scrambling, panting and making plaintive sounds in the back of his throat. She was gaining on him with each flight.

Realising this, he changed tack. He barrelled through a set of swing doors and was momentarily lost to Waller's sight again.

She followed him into a maze of passageways and doors, amplifying the audio receptors in her helmet with a flex of her fingers. She could hear his footsteps, so close that they could almost have been inside her head. Then the sharp crack of a door jamb. And voices, raised in fear and protest, guiding her to her prey.

He had forced his way into a flat. An elderly couple were sitting up in bed, scandalised, holding on to each other.

'Police,' rapped Waller in their direction. 'There's nothing to worry about. This is all really happening.'

She crossed the room in four strides. The geek had one foot out of the window, feeling for the fire-escape cage. Waller seized him by the overalls, micro-motors whining as she yanked him whimpering away from the sill and flipped him onto a table, which buckled under his weight. She hauled him back up and drove him into the wall, with a bit more force than was really necessary. As Steel always said, it was the only way to knock some sense into his kind.

She pulled the geek's hands behind him and bound his wrists with quick-set spray cuffs. 'Name,' she demanded, beaming with triumph.

'Alador Dragonheart, paladin of the northern kingdom of Etroria – but I will never betray the princess to orckind, you foul –'

She bounced his face off the wall. 'Reality check, pal!'

'P-please, p-please don't hurt us.'

Waller turned to see that the old couple were staring at her wide-eyed. More accurately, staring at their own reflections in her helmet visor. Trembling in their beds, as afraid of her as they had been of the geek. The man was trying to hush his wife, but she was babbling tearfully, 'We don't have many credits, b-but you can have them. Take everything. Just d-don't... don't... We have a grandson, you know. He's only t-two years old.'

Waller's good mood vanished in a second. A hot spring welled in her chest, and she pushed the geek aside and advanced on the couple angrily. 'Did you hear what I said?' she snapped. 'Did you? I told you there was nothing to worry about. Are you calling me a liar? Are you accusing an officer of the law of spreading fiction?'

The man was shaking his head desperately, dumbly, but the woman didn't know when to stop. 'N-no, of course not. It's just... we understand, we know how it w-works. Just name your price and it's yours. Anything. It just… We might need some time to p-pay, that's all, but we will. We will.'

Waller's eyes narrowed. 'You understand what? What have you seen?'

'N-nothing, I swear.'

'Then how can you know? What makes you think?' Her fingers twitched on the butt of her gun, and the old man found his voice at last.

'Please. My wife is a good woman. She doesn't imagine. She was confused, that's all. Tell her, Ailsa. Tell her.'

'I… please, I wouldn't have…' The woman sobbed. 'You can't accuse me of… I… we saw it. I know it was wrong, I know we shouldn't have watched, but it was real. I never… He told us.'

'*Who* told you, ma'am?' growled Waller. She knew the answer. She just needed to hear it, needed it to be real.

'Th-that man on the TV. Mr Gryden. Hal Gryden.'

She left her three prisoners stuck to the heating pipes and rode back down in the lift. She had called for a wagon, but it might take an hour to arrive – maybe longer, on a night like this – and she was too busy to wait. Anyway, they weren't going anywhere. Not without a solvent spray laced with the correct code sequence.

Waller stepped out onto the pavement and her jaw dropped open.

A man was leaning over her bike, apparently tinkering with the controls.

She blinked. She had to be confused. She closed her eyes and used the techniques she had been taught, breathing deeply, concentrating on what she could hear, taste, smell, feel, what was *real*. When she looked again, he was still there, in his non-regulation clothing – and while there was no law against that, it did mark him out as a potentially unsafe individual.

He had seen her and he met her gaze expectantly, one hand still lodged between the steering bar and the front shield. Waller went for her gun.

'All right, pal, step away from the vehicle. I said *step away from the vehicle*!'

He did as he was told, raising his hands, but he was grinning broadly. Far gone, she thought.

'Do you know the penalty for stealing police property?'

'I wasn't stealing it,' he protested. 'Anyway, it's OK. I'm with the government. An inspector.' He produced a card wallet from his pocket.

She advanced until she was facing him across the bike, her gun muzzle almost touching his chest. 'All right, that's enough, you keep those hands where I can see them. I'm taking you to see a doctor.'

'I'm *the* Doctor,' he said.

She edged her way around the bike towards him. He had given her no reason to shoot him yet, but he could snap at any moment. 'You are experiencing a delusional episode,' she explained to him slowly and clearly, 'but you can believe in me. Focus on my words and nothing else. I am Inspector Waller and I'm detaining you for your own protection.'

He was circling too, keeping the bike between them. 'Ah. What gave me away?'

'There is no government. Colony World 4378976.Delta-Four has had no government for three generations.'

'Is that what you think I said?'

'You said you were an inspector.'

'No, you said *you* were an inspector. I'm a researcher. For Channel… um, well look at the card.'

'I know what I heard.'

'And a moment ago you thought I was stealing your bike when I wasn't.'

'That was a reasonable extrapolation of future events based on past experiences and current indicators.'

'Well, then, there's your mistake. If you knew me –'

'"If" is a dangerous word, Doctor Whoever You Are.'

'I told you who I am. Look at the card.'

Waller looked at the card and for the briefest of moments she thought it was blank. Then the words and the holograph swam into focus, and she felt the itch in her brain again, like a warning. She forced herself to empty her mind, look at this stranger without preconceptions, concentrate only on what she could tell about him for sure. What she could prove.

He was about her age, maybe a little older. Cropped, dark hair, prominent nose and ears, inquisitive eyebrows. Wide blue eyes that held a gentle mocking quality. And he was a researcher, for 8 News.

'Did you bring a camera?' she asked, checking the sky for one of the floating orbs that tended to follow his sort around.

'That part comes later,' he said. 'For now, I'm asking questions, just trying to get a feel for the subject matter.'

'A documentary?'

'Of course. "Thought Crime on Our Streets". "The Fact of Fiction". I want to see what Inspector Waller goes through every day to hold back the nightmares. And we'll forget about that little mix-up just now, yeah? We all get a bit confused sometimes. Cheers.'

He had hopped onto the back seat of her bike, leaving Waller embarrassed and flustered.

'OK,' she said sternly, trying to regain her authority, 'you can ride out the shift with me and I'll answer your questions. Just don't get in my way.'

'Aye aye, Cap'n,' said the stranger enthusiastically. Waller froze with one hand on the steering bar, one foot in the air, and he started guiltily. 'Inspector, I mean. That was just a memory lapse. Not fiction.'

She regarded him suspiciously. His clothes were still a concern: the jacket in particular, cut from some sort of animal hide. But then, it was normal for media types to be a bit eccentric. All one step away from the Big White House, in her opinion.

She rummaged in the storage compartment, found a spare helmet and tossed it over her shoulder to him. Then, without waiting to see if he had donned it, she fired up the hoverjets and floored the accelerator.

She had reinserted the vidcom into the dashboard, allowing it to interface with the police bike's system. Its circular screen lit up again now with the image of Steel's strong face with its silver hair, square jaw and hard, grey eyes.

'It's him again, Waller. He's broadcasting.'

'Got a fix yet?' she asked.

'Still triangulating. We got lucky this time. I had people scanning all frequencies. We caught this one as soon as it started – and it looks like it's coming from your sector.'

'I won't let you down, Steel.'

'I know you won't. You're the best officer I have.' Steel glanced at something off-screen and his expression tightened into a cautious smile. 'We've got him. I'm *uploading the info to your 'com. Good luck, Waller. Steel out.'*

The screen turned green, and yellow programming symbols that Waller didn't understand flashed across it. Then the symbols were replaced by a big black arrow, which blinked insistently. It pointed dead ahead. This was it.

She felt a shiver of anticipation, but this too was dangerous. The best advice her mother had ever given her was that the most certain future was not yet fact.

'You enjoy your work, don't you?'

She had almost forgotten about her passenger. His voice came to her now clearly through the helmet radio, unhampered by the sounds of traffic and the rushing of air around them. 'Of course I do,' she said. 'It's the best job in the world. I'm saving people from themselves.'

'Yeah, that's not why you do it, though, is it? It's the uniform. The badge and the gun. The power that puts you above all those other drudges out there.'

She would have slung him off the bike there and then if she hadn't been concentrating on following the arrow. It swung to the right, and she wrenched the steering bar around, vaulted four rows of vehicles and caused a minor accident at the lights in her wake. 'No comment,' she answered tightly.

'Oh, that's good,' he said. 'I can use that in the programme. "No comment." That's very good. Some people would have told a white lie then, but you…'

'There are no white lies,' Waller growled. 'Just lies.'

'Sounds a bit harsh.'

'I'm a police inspector…' Waller fumbled for the stranger's name – she must have seen it on his card, but it wouldn't come to her. 'Er, Doctor. I see the damage done by fiction every day, the misery and the destruction. Oh yeah, it starts harmlessly enough. You hear the young people saying how it gives them a buzz, makes them forget their troubles for a while – but it never stops there. You know what I was doing when we met outside that residential building? Chasing down a cell of fantasists. They were gathering weekly in a cellar and – get this – swapping comic books!'

'Shocking!' agreed the Doctor. 'But – and I ask this purely in the line of business, you understand – what harm does it do, in fact?'

'You must have seen them: fiction geeks, sociopaths. They can't engage with reality, so they retreat ever deeper into unhealthy fantasies. Their behaviour becomes erratic, illogical. They see things that aren't there, react to imaginary threats. They become a danger to themselves and to others. It's best to stop the rot before it starts. Tolerate a lie, Doctor – any lie – and you open the way to madness.'

'No wonder there are no politicians,' said the Doctor. 'I bet they were the first up against the wall.'

'The government disbanded when we had no further need of it,' said Waller. 'Our laws were complete.'

'And of course they can't ever change.'

'Of course not. What are you suggesting?'

'Nothing at all. But some things can't be stated too often – and you put your case so well. I'm seeing potential here.'

Waller smiled at the compliment and noted at the same time that the arrow on the vidcom had turned a solid red. She was within two blocks of her target. 'You need material for your programme? Stick with me, pal. You're about to witness the biggest fiction bust this world's ever seen.' She leaned forward eagerly over the steering bar. Her palms were sweating beneath her gloves.

'One more question,' said the Doctor. 'What is this world called? I don't mean Colony World 890-whatever. I mean its name. It must have had one, once.'

Waller had to admit, he'd been a welcome distraction – at least with hindsight. He had kept her focused on the present. Now, though, she needed to concentrate on the task at hand. He was almost within her grasp. She could taste her victory.

'I don't know,' she shot back tersely. 'I don't want to know.'

But the Doctor persisted. 'You must have heard

something. A rumour. Something.'

'The original name of this world was abandoned,' she recited stiffly, 'when it was found to be problematic.'

'Problematic how? It can only have been a word or two.'

'But words have connotations, Doctor. Names have meanings, hidden below the surface. Sometimes they're just one step away from…'

'Fiction?'

She drowned out the question with a heartfelt curse. She steered her bike onto the pavement and jammed on the brakes, only the gravity cushion keeping her seated. She glared at the vidcom as if she could intimidate it into changing its mind. But the awful words were still displayed there, in block capitals: SIGNAL LOST.

'Something wrong?' asked the Doctor.

'I almost had him!' Waller howled.

'Who?'

'You heard what Steel said. He was broadcasting again. From here. We must be right on top of him. But…'

She cast around hopelessly. She could hardly begin to count the number of windows on this street alone. There were hundreds, thousands. There'd be officers swarming all over the area in minutes, but never enough of them. And they would be too late. They were always too late.

'I still don't know who you mean.'

'Gryden, of course. I mean Hal Gryden. The most dangerous man in the world.'

'Fantastic! But why?'

There was a new sound over the traffic. Ringing. An alarm. Waller cranked up her audio receptors again and pinpointed its origin. Just around the corner and half a block away. She kicked her bike back into gear and pulled out onto the roadway.

'You'll see,' she said grimly.

# THREE

here was a spyhole in the door. Rose stared out at
the distorted image of a short stretch of hotel
corridor. It was empty, as far as she could see. She
pressed her ear up to the wood. Nothing.

The footsteps had stopped a few minutes ago, but
she hadn't heard them go away.

This was nothing to do with her. It was probably
nothing at all.

But then, where was the Doctor?

Things had quietened down outside too. Rose
glanced back at the sleeping form of Captain Jack.
Was it worth waking him? She'd look daft if there *was*
nothing, just some drunk coming in late or looking
for the ice machine.

But then, the Doctor would have looked. And he
would have found something.

The decision was made. She opened the door.

The corridor *was* empty. Emboldened, Rose stepped out into it. It was dark and quiet. She jumped as the door clicked shut behind her. It was OK, though. It would unlock to her touch: they'd taken fingerprint scans at reception.

There was nowhere to hide. Just rows of doors. She must have been imagining things. Or she'd missed the sound of one of those doors opening and closing. Just a hotel guest, then, after all.

She smiled to herself, diffusing the tension that had built up inside her almost without her knowing it. She still wished she knew where the Doctor was. She hated it when he took off without her. He was probably just restless, though. Did he even sleep? If it'd been something big, he *would* have said.

The moment she turned her back, she heard noises. Rose whirled, catching her breath, feeling her pulse pounding in her neck.

A muffled thud. A clatter of wood against wood. A brief scraping. Now silence again, abrupt and deep.

There was a door in the opposite wall, just down the corridor. She took two, three cautious steps towards it, read the sign on it. It wasn't a room. She hadn't realised that before. It was a cleaner's store cupboard.

She wished she had a broom or something herself. She would have felt safer.

Whoever was in there, she thought, they were probably more afraid of her than she was of them.

That made sense, didn't it? Monsters don't go hiding in cupboards.

No, scratch that. In the Doctor's world, they probably did.

'I know you're in there,' she said, trying to sound brave. Jack was still within shouting distance. The stairs weren't far either and she was a good runner.

Rose took a deep breath, pulled open the cupboard door and leaped back in one motion.

She had revealed a skinny guy with sandy hair and a floppy fringe. About her age. He was cowering amid mops and buckets: surprisingly low-tech kit. No monsters, then. Rose let out her breath and grinned, and the guy responded, his own fearful expression softening into puzzlement.

'I was just, um…' He looked around the tiny cupboard, blinking fast, one hand circling vaguely.

'No, you weren't,' she said cheerfully.

'No. Um… no.'

The guy looked down guiltily, as if only just realising that he was holding something. It was a bundle of papers. He tried to shove it behind his back but caught his elbow on a mop handle and dropped the lot. He fell to his knees and scrambled to retrieve the scattered sheets. When Rose made to help, he became panic-stricken. He tried to mutter something about being able to cope, but the words got caught in his throat.

She grabbed a handful of sheets. The top one was filled with drawings. A comic strip, she realised. Over a sequence of six panels, an impossibly well-endowed young woman was chased through a medieval castle by ragged creatures that she described in a jagged word balloon as 'Brain-eating zombies!!!' She was cornered, at last, in a torture chamber, where she shrank into a corner, cupped her hands around her full red lips and screamed for a man to rescue her.

'You won't tell them, will you?' pleaded the skinny guy.

'Tell who what?'

'The cops. They're after me. Because of, you know, the fiction. They busted my reading group.'

'Reading group?' Rose looked at the other papers in her hand. There were a few more comic pages and a few sheets filled with neat, black text. 'You mean that's what all the racket was about? The sirens? All that, because you were... what? Just reading?' She remembered what the Doctor had said. 'Fiction!'

'It's not what it sounds like.'

'I don't care. I don't see what's wrong with it.'

A desperate hope shone in the young man's watery eyes. 'You... you don't mean... you don't *read* yourself?'

'Not...' Rose began, then stopped herself. She didn't want to seem thick. 'I mean, magazines and stuff, yeah.'

'Oh.' The guy looked disappointed. 'You mean non-fiction.'

'Mum didn't keep a lot of books about the flat when I was a kid, but I read at school. Sometimes. I'm Rose.'

He was staring at her, his jaw working soundlessly. Rose had to prompt him before he introduced himself. 'Domnic. Domnic Allen.'

She gave him back his papers. 'Where d'you get this stuff?' she asked.

'We…' He hesitated for a long moment, as if uncertain whether he could trust her. 'We write it. We write our own stories and swap them. Did. I mean, we *did* swap them. It was great to have an audience, to share my… my thoughts, even if it was only with a few people. It's over now.' A mournful look crossed his face. 'Nat was cut off by a police bike. I saw her. She'll be on her way to the Big White House. And the others… I have to contact them, find out if they… I don't know how I got away. I just kept running. Roach always kept us up to date on the best hiding places, the buildings you can get into without a code. This one, the hotel, it's a good one. You can get to the lifts without being seen from reception. I rode up as far as I could, then I didn't know what to do.' Rose opened her mouth to say something, but Domnic cut her off. 'Shush! Can you hear that?'

They listened for a moment and she shook her head. 'Nothing,' she mouthed.

'I thought I heard footsteps,' whispered Domnic, and Rose realised that he was trembling. 'On the stairs. Listen! Like cops, creeping up on us. They're trying to be quiet, but I can *hear* them. And… outside. That scratching sound. You must hear it. Tell me you can hear the scratching.' Again, Rose shook her head. 'They're climbing the walls. Using grapplers, probably hooking onto the fire-escape cage. They're surrounding us!'

There was a small, dirty window at the end of the corridor. Rose made for it, but Domnic threw himself into her path.

'Are you fantasy crazy? They'll see you! They'll see you and they'll know you've talked to me and they'll send you to the Big White House too!'

She hesitated and listened again. Still nothing. She was sure that Domnic was hearing things, that one look out of the window would prove it and calm his fears.

But what if he was right?

'OK,' she said decisively, 'you need a better place to hide than the cleaning cupboard. You're coming with me. No arguments.'

She grabbed him by the arm and propelled him back towards her room.

Jack was rubbing the sleep out of his eyes, sitting on the sofa in his boxers with his sheets draped over his lap. Domnic was kneeling in front of the TV: he had prised open a panel in the wall beside the flat screen and was messing with the tuning, filling the hotel room with white noise and the grey light of static.

'I'll show you,' he was muttering, seemingly to himself. 'If he's broadcasting, I'll find him. You'll see.'

Rose had spread Domnic's papers – his stories – out on the bed. 'Which of these is yours?'

'The comic strip,' he answered distractedly, over his shoulder.

'The zombies? It's… er, good. Well drawn. But you do know women don't really look like that? And if we did, we wouldn't *dress* like that.'

'It's stylistic. It's how they used to portray females in literature.'

'I s'pose, on the next page, the zombies tear off her clothes and she's rescued by some hunk and falls into his arms.'

Domnic broke off from what he was doing to turn and stare. 'You've studied the classics?'

'You can still *get* the, um, classics, then? They weren't all burnt or anything?'

'If you know where to look, which sites on the Ethernet. The data was all purged, but people have managed to reconstruct fragments: pages of old books, clips of movies and TV shows.' Domnic returned his attention to the TV as he continued, 'There was a bit of excitement last week. A whole script turned up. We're not sure, but the experts say it could be Shakespeare. He's, like, this guy who just wrote the best old films. This one is about a kid who goes to a school for wizards.'

'What are you doing exactly?' interjected Jack.

'Trying to find Static.' Catching Jack's raised eyebrow, Domnic clarified, 'With a capital S. It's a TV station – a pirate station – run by this guy called Hal Gryden. I was telling Rose about it. It broadcasts on different frequencies, at different times of the day. The cops would find it otherwise, you see, and they'd close it down, because it's making people think and that's the last thing they want. I'm surprised you haven't heard of it. Everyone's talking about it.'

'We've been out of town,' said Jack.

Domnic looked at him strangely. 'There *is* no "out of town".'

Rose thought she'd better fill Jack in on what he'd missed. 'The Doctor was right,' she said. 'Fiction is against the law here. You can't even tell a lie or they send you to a... a... what d'you call it?'

'A Home for the Cognitively Disconnected,' Domnic supplied. 'We call it – the main one – we call it the Big White House.'

'So be careful, you,' Rose teased Jack. 'None of your tall tales.'

'Dunno what you mean.' He affected a hurt expression as he pulled on his jeans. 'I have never spoken anything but the unvarnished truth in my whole life.'

'Yeah? Tell Domnic the one about the armoured walking sharks and the tin opener, see if he believes you. Go on!'

Domnic turned off the TV set with a disappointed sigh. 'Must be off-air.'

'What's so special about this Static channel anyway?' asked Jack.

'It's different, that's all. Do you know what the highest-rated show was on the official channels last month? That one about the accountants – you know, where they get kicked out of the firm one by one if they can't balance the books. It was real. It was dull! But Static… On Static there are drama plays like they made in the olden days, comedies to make you laugh and forget your problems, serials that leave you wondering what happens next.'

'Fiction,' Jack summarised.

Domnic's expression darkened. 'But there's fact in it too. Hal Gryden tells us how things are – how they *really* are – and how we can make them better. He opens our eyes, makes us look at the world in a different way.'

'Sounds like this Gryden guy's doing our job for us,' said Jack.

'You know the Doctor,' said Rose. 'He'll still want to be in the thick of things.'

'Guessing he is already. What I wanna know is how this happened – who told these people to stop dreaming, and why they listened.'

'They say it's dangerous to dream,' said Domnic, 'but it's exciting too. When I'm reading – or especially when I'm writing – it's like I can…' He struggled for the words. 'Like I'm living somewhere else, in a world where anything is possible. The characters, the monsters, the situations, they all seem real. And, yeah, I guess that's… I mean, sometimes I feel as if I could get pulled into that world, and that scares me. But it's worth it because… because when I'm there, it feels like that other world is in colour, and when I come back to this one, it's all black and white.'

Domnic blinked and suddenly looked at Rose and Jack as if he had said too much.

'Any idea where we find this Hal Gryden?' asked Jack.

'Why?'

'Like I said, we're on the same wavelength – only Gryden seems to be set up to do some real good.'

Domnic shrugged. 'No one knows. They say he was a businessman once, really successful – had four cars and a luxury apartment in Sector One-Alpha, the works. But he's had to go into hiding. If the cops caught up with him, he'd spend the rest of his life in the Big White House.'

'He must have a studio,' said Rose.

'Dozens of them. They say he used his fortune to build studios all over the city. He never broadcasts from the same place two days running. I wish I *could* find him. I dream of being able to write for him, having my stories seen by millions. Can you imagine that? I used to think… No, no, it's silly…'

'Go on,' said Rose encouragingly.

'I thought, maybe, through the reading group… There were only a few of us, but I thought, some day, if one of my stories could get back to *him* somehow… I just… I want to do something more, you know, worthwhile than… than calling up people on the vidphone to sell them windows.'

'You're a salesman?' Jack piped up. 'Hey, that needs imagination too. Best way to close a deal is to spin your customer a good story.' He turned to Rose with a grin. 'Did I tell you about the time I was out of fuel in the Ataline System? All I had was a traffic cone I'd picked up on a night out. I had to persuade this old prospector it was worth the price of a bag of caesium rocks. I told him it was the crown of –'

Domnic looked at him sharply. 'What are you trying to say? We don't lie to the customers. We wouldn't be… I mean, we just don't! We tell them about the product, what it can do, that's all.'

'He didn't mean anything by it,' said Rose, puzzled by the sudden change of mood.

'Look, I… I… Just forget everything I said. It was

only thoughts, that's all. I'm not a writer. I don't know where those things, those stories, came from. I just... I found them. Outside. I was confused for a while, but I feel better now.' He had got to his feet and was edging towards the door as he spoke.

Rose stood too and got in his way. 'C'mon, what about that stuff you were saying? Worlds in colour and writing for TV and all that? Now suddenly that doesn't matter any more? I know it does, Domnic.'

'It's all this... this talk of armoured sharks and crowns and... and schools where you read fiction. I think you're... If you want to know, I think you're both far gone. Fantasy crazy. I think you should see a...'

'Y'know,' said Rose, 'real life doesn't have to be in black and white. A friend of mine taught me that. You should meet him.'

'... doctor.'

'Eh? How did you –'

'You mentioned a...' Domnic's eyes widened with fright and he backed away from Rose as far as he could in their cramped confines. 'Is that why you're asking me all these questions? You're police, aren't you? You... you're working with the doctors at the Big White House, and you're trying to trick me, pretending to be sympathetic.'

Jack looked scandalised. 'Everywhere I go today, people are calling me a liar.'

'Just today?' teased Rose.

Then Domnic made a run for the door – and, when Rose stopped him again, he let out a wail of frustration and snatched the nearest object to hand, which was a grotty old kettle. 'Let me past! Let me go or I'll brain you, I swear I will!'

'No, you won't,' said Rose, trying to sound calm, holding her hands out in front of her in a steadying gesture. She wasn't altogether sure of her ground, but the kettle was empty and it didn't look heavy, and she doubted that Domnic was all that strong. If he did attack her, she could defend herself.

Jack came up behind Domnic and placed a hand on his shoulder. 'Cool it, fella,' he said firmly. 'No one's lying to you, and no one's trying to --'

He never finished the sentence. Domnic pushed past him, taking him by surprise with a strength born of desperation. Before Rose or Jack could react, he was at the window, wrenching it open. The room was filled with the noise of traffic and the curtains danced in a soft wind. 'I won't go to that place!' vowed Domnic. 'I've heard what they do to you there, how they… how they burn out parts of your brain, so you can't think at all. Well, I'd rather die!'

Rose's heart leaped as she realised what he was going to do. She took a step back, groping for the words that would reassure him, convince him that they meant him no harm.

But Domnic had one foot over the ledge and Jack was hurtling across the room, realising that there was no time for words, and all Rose could think was that they were sixty floors up and no one could survive a drop like that.

Jack lunged towards Domnic, but his arms closed on thin air. He turned back to Rose, his ashen face telling the story.

The colours of the TV screen outside flickered in the empty square behind him.

Domnic had jumped.

# FOUR

It was easy enough to pinpoint the source of the disturbance.

There were lights in the first-floor windows of an office block and people popping out of the entrance doors below: men in identical black dinner jackets and women in identical white cocktail dresses. Some of them were hysterical.

Caught up in the chase, Inspector Waller hadn't paid much attention to her surroundings until now. She hadn't realised she was at the edge of the financial district, one of the more affluent sectors. Its buildings looked the same as all others from the outside.

The rich people were partying – and if the lights were still shining at this time of the morning, it must have been a good one.

She braked, feeling her bike's centre of gravity shift as the Doctor leaped from the back seat before they had reached a full stop. He flung his helmet aside and placed himself obdurately in the way of the runners.

'He's in the ballroom,' they jabbered over the clamour of the traffic and the alarm bell. 'He has a –'

'– knife –'

'– a gun –'

'– a satellite in orbit with death rays programmed to wipe out this sector –'

'– wearing an iron mask –'

'– rays shooting out of his eyes –'

'– wants to take over the –'

'– entire bank –'

'– universe –'

'– the title of Mr Cosmic Champion of the World –'

Waller grabbed the Doctor's arm and pulled him away from them. 'No point talking to them. They've had a shock. They're delusional.'

Some of the revellers were scrambling over the hoods of stalled cars in their attempts to get as far away as they could. Some drivers abandoned their vehicles to flee alongside them on foot, caught up in the panic.

Waller and the Doctor raced into the building. Immediately, the traffic sounds were calmed. They were surrounded by marble, lush jungle plants and soft lighting. A fountain gurgled in a soothing rhythm, but the alarm bell was still ringing, like a drill in Waller's head.

A dinner-jacketed man with a weasel face skidded up to her. He was holding a banana like a gun. 'About time you got here,' he panted. 'I got the perps pinned down on the first floor – they crashed a dinner dance for the Sector One Bank, but they didn't count on my being here. I've got ten men round the back and four more ready to come through the windows at my –'

She gave him a backhand slap, which sent him reeling.

'Feel better now, do you?' asked the Doctor.

'He'll thank me in the morning. You'd best stay here.' Waller attacked a flight of stairs that swept up to what had to be the ballroom entrance. 'This could be serious and I can't be responsible for your sanity.'

The Doctor didn't argue. He just ignored her.

They barrelled through the doors, raising a collective gasp from the crowd inside. Waller had her gun drawn and was scanning a sea of black and white, looking for a tell-tale splash of colour. It wasn't hard to find.

He was standing on a table in the centre of the room, apparently oblivious to the fact that he had one foot in a bowl of trifle. A middle-aged man, overweight and red-cheeked, his hair dark and greasy. He was brandishing a small black control device, and at the sight of the new arrivals he waved it petulantly and warned, 'Not a step closer. Don't you come a step closer or I'll blow this place sky high!'

'That's what you get for barging in without looking,' said the Doctor, and Waller was alarmed to see that he was grinning like a loon. 'I do it all the time.'

She felt ice in her stomach. This had gone beyond a few lies. This was what Inspector Waller had long feared but tried not to imagine. How many times had she said to Steel that something like this was coming? How many times had he agreed with her? Such foreknowledge gave her no comfort now, though.

It was her job to evaluate this new threat, to consider the worst-case scenario. But she had encountered nothing like this before and all the possible futures from this point on felt like fiction to her.

Whenever she thought about it – as her mind edged towards that dangerous area – the whole world seemed to explode into flame, and Waller could smell smoke and hear the screams of the burning, and that damned itch was flaring up in the back of her brain until she wanted to tear open her skull to get at it.

*Eyes closed. Breathe deeply. Hold it together. You've come too far to let it all fall apart again.*

She was only dimly aware that the fat geek was talking. His tone was petulant but edgy, his head jerking around as he tried to keep the whole room in sight at once. 'OK, no one else comes in and no one else leaves. I mean it. Anyone goes near a door, you'll be sorry. Now, everyone on the floor! Go on, down! You have to do as I say, or I'll blow you all up. I will!'

There were about forty hostages, Waller reckoned. Forty lives at stake, not to mention the property damage. Maybe not only to this building; maybe to the entire block. And the cars outside and anyone still in the surrounding office buildings and… and… Her brain was itching, buzzing, and she couldn't think about it.

'Yeah, yeah, go on. That's it, down on the floor. Down in the dirt. Grovel to me! Grovel, like I had to grovel to you all these years! And you – you get that head down, Jankins, before I remember how you got that promotion by taking the credit for my work. And Miss Lieberwitz – I saw what you wrote about me, don't think I didn't. Well, I'll show you "unstable".'

The bankers were obeying, one by one, in dreadful silence. Waller seethed and fretted, fingering her gun, knowing it was no use to her. She needed time to get her thoughts straight. The geek shot her a pointed glare and she dropped the weapon, showing her empty hands as she lowered herself onto her stomach.

Surreptitiously, she flipped a switch on her wrist-mounted vidcom. There'd be bikes en route already, answering the alarm – but now they'd know there was an officer in danger and they'd hear everything that went on in here.

'You might well look at me like that, Suzi Morgan,' the fat geek ranted. 'I used to like you. You could have been one of the people I let go – but you know why you weren't, don't you? Do the words "parking space" mean anything to you? Do I deserve nothing after thirty-two years? Do I? Well, you – all of you – are the ones who have to beg *me* now.'

'Or you'll kill everyone in this room.'

The Doctor was still standing. The alarm bell cut out almost on cue, so that his cheerful words were the only sound to be heard, electrifying the sudden hush.

'Starting with yourself.'

'Doctor,' hissed Waller, grabbing at his ankle in an attempt to bring him down, 'this is no time to go fantasy crazy!'

'Stand up, Waller,' he said sternly. 'We can hardly have a conversation with you flat on your face, and that's all matey here wants – isn't that right?'

'I… I…' the fat geek stammered. 'I just want someone to… to notice me.'

'Done that. I can safely say you've got our full attention. Now, what's so important?'

The Doctor wasn't crazy. He was a genius. He was bringing the geek down to earth, making him concentrate on the logic, the fact, of his actions. He was doing what Waller should have done, and she smarted at the realisation.

'Come on,' he chided, 'we've not got all day.'

Then he blew it in a second, with one careless question. The one that Waller had been trained never, ever to ask.

'What do you want?'

She leaped to her feet. 'Don't you dare answer that!'

The geek's eyes widened and he thrust the detonator towards her. But there was no going back now. She had to talk him down, before the Doctor could do any more harm. Forget the explosives, forget the consequences if she got this wrong. Just treat this geek as she'd treat any other.

'That's what got you into this mess,' she said firmly. 'Wanting, dreaming, imagining. You've got a job, haven't you? You can afford a flat and a TV and food. You should think about that, not about what others might have. Sure, there are people with better jobs and more money than you, but that's life. Deal with it!'

'And you think this is the right approach, do you?' murmured the Doctor.

'Listen…' began Waller more kindly, leaving a significant pause.

'Arno Finch,' said the geek in a small voice.

'Arno, I know you can't have meant for all this. I mean, when you look at what you're doing in the light of reality, it must seem… well, I bet it's hard to believe, isn't it? It must seem like fiction. Because people don't plant bombs in their workplaces or threaten entire city blocks in real life, do they? Especially not people like you, Arno – people who've worked hard and obeyed the law their whole life. I know *I've* never seen it. I'm a police inspector and I've never seen anything like this. How about you, Arno? Have you ever seen it?'

'I… don't know. Maybe. I think… yeah, I think I saw…'

'No, Arno. In real life, I said. Think! I know it's hard to tell fact from fiction, but think! When you saw this before, when you saw someone behaving like this, you were in your flat, weren't you? You were watching the telly.'

'News,' moaned Arno Finch. 'It must have been… I can't remember, but it must have been on the news.'

'If it'd been on the news, Arno, we'd all know about it. I think you've been watching something else. You've been watching Static, haven't you?'

'No! No, I wouldn't!'

'It's all right, Arno, it's not all your fault. You're changing channels one day and Hal Gryden comes on, and you've heard so much about him and he's saying things that you want to be true, and you're curious. But you have to understand that that man has made you sick. Hal Gryden is fantasy crazy, Arno – and you know how fiction spreads. You're doing it yourself. You're making people afraid, making them imagine the future, and you know where that leads. As it is, everyone in this room – even the people you let go – will need counselling. They'll probably have to shut the bank down. You've got your revenge, Arno.'

'I just… No. Not until they say they're sorry. Not until they promise to… to treat me better. Move my desk closer to the… the…'

'They can't, Arno. You're a bright man, you know how things are. We're only a small world. Our resources are stretched to the limit. There's no more. You have to accept that. Concentrate on the fact and forget the rest, the static.'

'But… but no, that's not true, because I've seen people, normal people like me, and they were answering questions and being given… m-money and cars and… and holidays away from this place.'

Waller shook her head, pitying him even as she despised his weakness. He wasn't the villain here. The villain had done his work, beaming his corrupting ideas into this fool's brain, and he was long gone. 'I've heard about shows like that – but they're fiction too, Arno. Just like the ones that tell you not to trust the police when you know you can. You ever meet someone who's been on one of these question shows? Anyone who's won one? Can you prove they're real?'

He was sweating and shaking. He was about to

make his choice: either give up or do something stupid.

'No. You can't. Then they *aren't* real, are they?' She took a step towards him, hoping her physical presence would ground him, reassure him. Or just intimidate him – she didn't mind which. As long as he was thinking about nobody, nothing, else.

The geek let out a plaintive wail and tried to back away from her.

The trifle bowl slipped out from under him, and he toppled backwards off the table and fell out of Waller's sight.

Her heart leaped into her mouth. She sprang forward, straining her micro-motors to the limit, knowing it was already too late.

Time seemed to freeze, possibilities suspended unrealised.

And then the room exploded and didn't explode.

It was as if Waller was living in two worlds at once, one overlaid upon the other. She could see the ballroom intact at the same time as it was blasted apart. Her way to the geek was clear and yet filled with falling, flaming masonry. People were screaming and crying and yelling for help, and that was the same in both realities.

It was just like before.

Only this time she could fight it, because she knew what it was.

The explosives had detonated/hadn't detonated. One was fact, one fiction. Waller didn't have to know which was which. In the first case, she could do nothing. The ceiling had fallen in and she was pinned. In the second…

She ignored the pains in her limbs that may or may not have been real. She vaulted over the table on which the fiction geek had been standing. She found him on his back, whimpering to himself. His eyes bulged as he saw her and he made to activate the detonator but realised he had dropped it.

Waller and the geek lunged for the black box in unison. Twenty fingers fought to be the first to close around it, but it skittered away from them all. It was brought to a halt by a battered brown shoe.

Waller's world lurched again as she looked up, not knowing what she would see, half expecting to blink and find she was trapped in the rubble, bleeding.

The Doctor scooped up the detonator, glanced at it and said cheerfully, 'TV remote control.' He flung it over his shoulder and dropped to his haunches beside them. 'Thought so, but I couldn't be sure. I had the sonic screwdriver ready to block the radio signal.' He gave Arno Finch an almost congratulatory slap on the shoulder. 'But you were just having us on, weren't you?'

His presence was like an anchor, pulling Waller back to sanity.

The nightmare fell away and she let out a breath of relief as she knew at last that the worst hadn't happened. She was alive – they were all alive – the building was intact and the geek was beneath her, the struggle knocked out of him. But what had the Doctor just said…?

There were no bombs! Why hadn't she realised? She had been so quick to accept that fiction, to believe in something she couldn't see for herself. She had forgotten the first rule.

Angry with herself, she rolled the geek over and spray-cuffed his wrists behind his back. 'It's the Big White House for you, pal,' she snarled, 'and I hope they fry your brain for what you've done to these people, you pervert!'

She regretted her harsh words almost immediately, regretting even more the fleeting truth in them. She *did* understand, beneath her frustration. She had sought out the Static channel herself once, on a cold, lonely night. She had just wanted to see. She had been lucky. She hadn't found it. The difference between her and the Arno Finches of this world, the fantasy crazy, was more slender than she cared to admit.

'Y-you'll tell them, won't you?' the geek stammered, tears in his eyes. 'You'll tell them it wasn't my fault. I was just… just doing what they said on the TV.' The Doctor leaned over him and muttered something in his ear. Waller didn't catch the words, but they seemed to calm the geek down a little.

The bankers were picking themselves up, adjusting to their new reality – those who could. Too many were still on the ground, curled into foetal balls, sobbing.

'You see what I mean now?' Waller said to the Doctor.

'Yeah, I do.'

'This is what Gryden does. This is why he's so dangerous. This TV station of his, it's making people greedy, teaching them to disrespect authority.'

'Yeah, it is.'

'He's driving them crazy!'

'I've misjudged you, Inspector Waller. I thought you were the monster here.'

He bounced to his feet while Waller was still gaping. 'There are no monsters, Doctor,' she spluttered.

'Yeah, there are,' he said. 'Some of them are just better at hiding than others. And then there're the ones we wouldn't know if we saw them. C'mon, we're going.'

He set off at a jog as if he expected Waller to follow – and somehow, maddeningly, she found herself doing just that.

'Where to?' she cried after him, helplessly.

'Big White House,' he called back over his shoulder. 'I want to see what happens next.'

# FIVE

"S cuse me, guv, you got a credit for a cold beer?'
Captain Jack hadn't seen the tramp slumped in a
nest of cardboard in the doorway of a boarded-up
shop. He'd been distracted by an advertising hoarding
across the street, on which a tin of toothpaste was
depicted beside the slogan 'Not Quite as Effective at
Plaque Removal as the Market Leader, But It Costs a
Bit Less'. He was beginning to see what Domnic had
meant about the problems of selling on this world.

'I'm having these visions, see, keep dreaming I'm
one of them rich businessmen. I need the booze to
numb my brain before I go fantasy crazy.'

Jack grinned. 'I like your sales pitch.'

The tramp looked up at him, forlorn in his layers of
tatty clothing. 'Just telling the truth, guv. Wouldn't
have me do less, would you?'

'I got no cash, though, sorry.' The tramp looked so

downcast that Jack couldn't help but reach out to him. 'Here, come with me. I'll get you a meal and a hot drink or something.'

'Rather have a beer. Thought you said you had no money.'

'I'll use my imagi – I mean, I'll find a way.'

The tramp took the proffered hand and let Jack lift him to his feet. He was shorter than the American and his stooped shoulders made him seem shorter still. He was getting on a bit, his hair thinning and his beard white, but his eyes were bright and alert.

'Knew you'd help me, guv,' he wheezed gratefully, 'soon as I saw your clothes. You're not one of the drones. You're a thinker. I'm a thinker too.'

Jack just nodded, remembering the last 'thinker' he had encountered.

He remembered the horror he'd felt as Domnic had leaped out of his grasp – at knowing it would take the young man long, agonising seconds to die and that he could do nothing but watch him fall.

Then Domnic's flailing hand had hit the anti-gravity updraught of the fire-escape cage, attached to the wall a few metres away, and horror had turned to amazement.

His momentum had been stolen. Drifting like a feather, Domnic had somersaulted into the confines of the cage's three vertical bars. Then he had fallen again, faster than before but with the promise of a gentle landing.

Jack had had all of two seconds to think about following, but the leap was too far: the cage was meant to be accessed from the roof, not from here. Suicidal he may not have been after all, but Domnic had still taken one hell of a risk.

Jack couldn't work out why. One moment, he'd been happy to talk, apparently glad to have found two kindred spirits. The next... It was as if he'd become paranoid, imagining the worst of them and believing it. As if the people who ran this world were right and dreams *were* dangerous.

Perhaps they were, to people unused to dreaming.

The sun was rising over the grey buildings, but it was a cold day and the sky was heavy with cloud. The roads were clogged as usual, and the pavements were packed too: people with grey jumpsuits and grey faces, keeping their heads down as they marched to work. The hoverjets of stalled vehicles kicked up grey dust, which swirled around the pedestrians' ankles. Domnic was right, thought Jack: this was a black and white world.

'I'm looking for someone,' he said. 'Hal Gryden. Runs a TV station. Heard of him?'

The tramp shrugged. 'You won't find many as haven't heard of Hal Gryden. Probably seen him too, if they're honest. They say his son was picked up on a minor storytelling charge, sent to the Big White House. Took his own life, he did. That's why Gryden hates the system.'

That tallied with what Jack already knew. After Domnic had run off into the night, he and Rose had spent two hours surfing the Ethernet back at the hotel, in a little cubbyhole behind reception. The night manager had given them a code card and added a charge to their account. They'd found an address for Domnic Allen easily enough, and thousands of mentions of Hal Gryden, but no concrete information. If he *had* been a businessman as Domnic had claimed, if he'd ever had a listed address or a vidphone number, they could find no trace of it.

'Hal Gryden. That can't be his real name, can it?'

'Reckon not,' said the tramp. 'So they say, anyway. I hear a lot, I do. Keep my ear to the ground.'

'You ever hear his real name? Or how to find him?'

'Saw him on the info-screen at the end there, few weeks ago. He cut in on RTV 4 for a minute. Bounced his signal off their own satellite, so they say. Clever fellow. You ask me, if anyone can save this world it's him.'

'Everyone must know his face,' said Jack. 'How can he hide?'

'You get me a beer, I'll tell you everything I know.'

'You old fraud!' Jack grinned. 'You don't know a thing, do you?'

'I tell no word of a lie, guv.'

'Where do you get a beer round here, anyway?'

'Pub.'

'At this time of the morning?'

'Open all hours. Alcohol's good, in the right dosage. Numbs the brain, saves us thinking too hard, keeps us sane. Keeps things real. There's a decent place just round the corner.'

'OK,' said Jack. 'Lead on.'

As dawn had turned the sky red, Rose had crashed out in their room. She would catch up on a few hours' sleep, then go and find Domnic. With luck, the Doctor would be back before she left. If not... well, that was one more thing to worry about.

In the meantime, Jack was left to find one man in a city – a world – of twenty million, according to the Ethernet. He didn't fancy his chances. Unless he did something that Domnic had inadvertently suggested. Something risky.

This, then, was his mission. To tell stories. Ask questions. Draw attention. Make a name for himself.

And make Hal Gryden come to him.

An hour and a half later, Captain Jack was in his element, perched on a bar stool with a semicircle of rapt faces in front of him: tired nightshift workers and dispossessed unemployed, who'd been wallowing in their own misery before his arrival.

'So this poor guy walks into the refectory all dressed up like the Face of Boe, with the admiral standing right there. You should have seen him when he realised it wasn't a costume party at all. He didn't know where to put his... well, his whole body.'

He leaned back against the bar and took a swig from his bottle, revelling in his audience's appreciative laughter.

It hadn't been like this in the first bar. The customers there, all sitting in silence at their tables in the gloom, had just glowered at him. One couple had plugged their ears and started to sing loudly. Someone else had thrown a bottle at him and called him a 'fiction geek'. The second place he had been thrown out of by a surly bartender almost as soon as he had opened his mouth.

Not that he was short of hecklers here. 'You should go see a doctor, you should,' snapped a sharp-featured old woman from the other end of the bar. 'And the rest of you oughtn't to be egging him on.'

'It's the truth, I swear,' said Jack.

'I believe him,' piped up another patron, wiping tears of mirth from his eyes. 'I don't reckon there's anyone could make up stuff like this.'

'Yeah? What about that Hal Gryden?'

The old woman had found a supporter. 'If you're telling the truth,' he challenged Jack, brandishing a glass, 'where's your ship? Why didn't we see it landing?'

'It's out in the jungle, and it didn't land. It

materialised. Yeah, you heard me,' said Jack, raising his voice above the renewed gales of laughter. 'I came here in a time/space capsule. From the outside, it looks like something called a police box. They had them on Earth in the twentieth century, but this one's bigger on the inside.'

The old woman slammed her glass down and spluttered, 'You expect anyone to believe that?'

'It's OK, ma'am,' Jack called after her as she made a show of storming out, 'you can listen. The police can't touch us because this isn't fiction. It's my life!'

'Prove that to the doctors!' she spat as a parting shot.

'Tell us about this capsule of yours,' someone requested.

'Oh, it's not mine,' said Jack. 'It belongs to this guy called… Well, I'm not sure you're ready for that one yet.' He affected a mournful look at his empty bottle, which had the desired effect. A cute blond builder type stepped up to buy him another. 'And one for my friend,' requested Jack cheerfully. He turned to the table in the corner with a thumbs-up gesture, but it was empty. He frowned and surveyed the crowd, seeing the tramp only as he appeared at his elbow.

'Reckon it's time we left, Cap'n,' he muttered.

'You kidding me? I'm just warming up. And I got us another –'

'There'll be other places,' hissed the tramp fiercely,

'but not if we hang around this one. The old bat –
she'll be on her vidphone to the police by now.'

Jack practically fell off his stool in his haste to
stand. The old man was right. He'd have seen it
himself if it hadn't been for the booze. He'd only
meant to have one, just to get in the mood. Soft
drinks only in the next pub, he swore.

'I've just been reminded,' he announced, 'of a
pressing appointment. It's been cool speaking to you
all, and if anyone comes looking for me – apart from
the police, I mean – I'm staying at –'

'Just tell them to look in the static,' the tramp
interrupted hastily.

Jack gave the old man a protesting look as he was
taken by the arm and led to the door, to the
disappointed groans of his audience.

'What did you do that for?' he complained, blinking
in the daylight.

'You want the police down on you?' asked the
tramp.

'Who cares? Anyway, no one would have talked.
They'd have nothing on me.'

'How much do you think they need?'

'And I'm meant to be getting attention. I want to be
found.'

'By Hal Gryden,' the tramp reminded him, 'no one
else. And he'll find you if he wants to. You ever seen
him on the TV? He knows what goes on. He's got eyes

and ears everywhere. He wants to find you, Cap'n, he'll find you – trust me on that one.'

It was early afternoon as they made their escape from Jack's fourth successful recital. They used the back door.

He had been feeling pretty pleased with himself. Already, his reputation was preceding him. He was being applauded on sight, recognised by his dress sense alone, and was finding more and more people eager to listen to him. In a world starved of stories, Jack supposed they spread all the more quickly.

And they kept on spreading. 'Tell us the one about the armoured sharks!' someone had shouted from the back of this latest, biggest crowd.

Even if he didn't find Gryden, he was doing some good. He was doing what the Doctor had wanted: introducing fiction to this world.

Not that his stories were fiction exactly. He had continually had to reassure people that they were hearing only the truth, and indeed they were. Well... give or take the odd embellishment. You had to keep them interested, after all.

Nevertheless, he was engaging their imaginations, expanding their horizons beyond their dull little planet. And in the process he was sticking it up an unjust authority... Life didn't get much better than this.

Jack was loving every second of his new-found fame. That was why, this time, he had stayed too long.

They were racing down a garbage-strewn alley, hemmed in by high walls from which the sounds of police sirens echoed until he had no idea which way they were coming from. The tramp was showing a surprising turn of speed, especially considering how much he'd drunk.

'You should leave me,' insisted Jack. 'No need for us both to get nicked.'

'Enough people have seen us together,' the tramp reasoned. 'I'm an accessory before and after the fiction. Anyway, I know these alleyways like the back of my hand. No way you're getting out of this one without me, Cap'n.'

Jack didn't argue as the tramp led him around a corner.

Into the path of a police bike.

It was charging towards them like an enraged rhinoceros, all armour plating. For an instant, the tramp was frozen in its harsh blue light, but Jack grabbed his hand and pulled him along. Towards the oncoming vehicle.

He had seen a gap in a row of rusted railings. He pushed the tramp through and scrambled after him, as the bike screeched past and came to a sudden, anti-gravity-assisted halt. Its rider leaped from the saddle, an imposing figure in his black armour and face-concealing helmet.

They were on a patch of wasteland, piled high with abandoned electronic goods. Jack seized a burned-out washing machine on a set of castors and set it rolling up to the railings as the cop tried to squeeze his padded shoulders through after them. He recoiled as the machine hit. It would delay him for a moment.

Jack leaped over a clapped-out robo-butler and found cover behind a mound of assorted junk. The tramp took the long way round, and joined him wheezing and gasping for breath. He didn't pause, though, or complain. His eyes were alight with excitement. He was running on adrenaline. For now.

He wasn't the only one. 'We need somewhere to lie low,' said Jack. 'As soon as that cop calls in our location, they'll move in to surround us.'

The tramp didn't say anything. He took the lead as they threaded their way through more junk heaps on a seemingly random course.

And suddenly the cop was there, a good distance away but fortuitously in the right spot at just the right time for a clear line of sight. He snapped off four gunshots, and Jack yanked the tramp back out of the path of the fizzing blue energy bullets.

They plunged back into the junk heap maze, turned left, left, right, and then the tramp was scrambling to climb a rotten wooden fence twice his height. Jack gave him a boost before attacking the fence at a run. His hands found the top, and his companion helped to pull him up and over.

They dropped onto a muddy incline, the tramp losing his balance and slipping and sliding until Jack caught him. He had almost toppled headlong into a rusty red river, which wended its way sluggishly between weed-choked banks.

They ran on, roots tearing at their ankles, overlooked by the boarded-up windows of old warehouses. They came to a spot where wooden crates had been dumped in the water, providing a series of precarious stepping points to the far side. A short way beyond that the river divided and they followed the right fork until finally they came to a halt beneath an iron bridge.

The tramp's spurt of energy had deserted him and he sank to the ground, his knees to his forehead, breath rattling in his lungs. 'They won't think to look for us down here,' he panted. 'Not for a while. Most of them don't know about the river. They built right over it, you see.' His words were almost swallowed by the thundering of traffic above their heads.

'That was a close one,' remarked Jack, when they had both got their breath back. 'From now on, we'll have to move on faster, never stay in one place too long.'

The tramp shook his head. 'You can't go out there

again, Cap'n. Not dressed like that. The cops have your description. There'll be bikes out all over the sector.'

'I'm not gonna hide. I told you, I want to be found.'

'You have been. He knows where you are. He's always known.'

Jack frowned. 'What are you...'

The tramp climbed to his feet. 'You wanted to get attention? You've been doing that since you arrived on this world, you and your friends. I knew where you were staying. I was just waiting in that doorway for one of you to come by.'

Jack laughed. 'I get it. Eyes and ears everywhere. You're one of them, aren't you? You work for him. You're some sort of scout. You've been testing me.'

'Not quite true, Cap'n.' The tramp straightened his shoulders for the first time and drew himself up to his full height, meeting Jack's gaze with a gleam in his eyes and a smile on his lips. 'I *am* him. I'm the man you've been looking for. I'm Hal Gryden.'

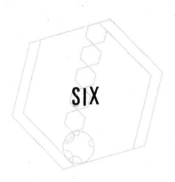

# SIX

The doctors will tell you that all fiction is harmful, that the pleasure we find in good dreams is more than offset by the terror when those dreams go bad. I say that even the bad dreams are good for us.

Rose couldn't place the voice. She squirmed in her bed, defiantly keeping her eyes closed, hoping it would go away and leave her alone.

There's something alluring about monsters, about things that hide at the foot of your bed and go bump in the night. If there weren't, we wouldn't dream about them. We want to experience that thrill, taste that fear.

She'd nodded off and left the telly on again. It was a wonder her mum hadn't burst in to unplug it, whingeing about the electric meter.

*There's nothing wrong with a healthy scare. It sets our hearts racing, unleashes our adrenaline, lets us know we're alive.*

She was surfacing from sleep, despite her efforts, remembering where she was.

*For after all, what could be more exciting – more stimulating – than tackling those monsters head on?*

She'd been lying awake again, the chorus of rush-hour horns from the street below blasting in her ears. She'd turned on the TV to drown them out and found it tuned to the static between channels where Domnic had left it.

The white noise itself had been comforting: a bit harsh, maybe, but a constant regular sound to blot out all others. Rose's eyelids had sagged and she'd let the sound draw her into darkness.

*In our dreams, we can do that. We can have that excitement, and yet be protected. Our dreams can't hurt us.*

What time was it? How long had she slept? Was the Doctor back yet?

What was she listening to?

*This has been an editorial on behalf of Static TV. I'm Hal Gryden. We're forced to cease broadcasting now, but we'll be back this afternoon with our play for today:* Castle of the Brain-eating Zombies. *Look for us in the static.*

Wide awake now, Rose sat bolt upright. She was just in time to catch a fleeting impression of a face on the TV screen before it was buried in a grey snowstorm. She leaped out of bed and went for the tuning controls, which Domnic had left exposed.

She scrolled through a dozen channels, finding the usual procession of newsreaders and narrated documentaries.

She lingered on the live feed from a courtroom, where a woman was petitioning for divorce on the grounds that her husband had destroyed her confidence with a campaign of malicious lies: '*He specifically and repeatedly assured me that my bum did not look big in that dress, and yet when I arrived at the restaurant –*'

She turned off the telly and looked at the clock. She couldn't make head or tail of the six numbers on its face. She didn't know which way round to read them, or even how many hours there were in a day on this world. But a glance out of the window told her that the sun was standing high in the sky.

And still no Doctor. She pulled on her jacket and found her mobile in the pocket: the one he'd gimmicked so that it never needed recharging and showed a signal anywhere, any time. She thought there might be a text or a missed call from him. No dice, though. One day, she was gonna make him carry his own phone – she knew he had one, when it suited him.

He'd find her. He always did. In the meantime, she should get on with it. Find Domnic. Rose and Jack had agreed he could be useful to them, if they could calm him down. He could be their local guide. Anyway, she wanted to make sure he was OK after last night's freakout.

She scribbled a quick message for the Doctor – just in case – and was headed for the door when she heard a noise behind her.

A footstep, where there had been nobody a second ago.

Rose spun around, catching her breath.

The room was empty.

She smiled to herself. She was glad the Doctor and Captain Jack hadn't seen her, jumping at shadows.

But just for a second there… Just for a second – and her smile froze at the recollection – she had been convinced, absolutely convinced, that she wasn't alone. That there had been someone – no, some*thing* – behind her.

And not just anything. A…

She could hardly bring herself to think the word. But the image was there, clear in her mind. A white-faced creature in ragged clothes. Peeling skin, vacant eyes, arms reaching limply for her as if they were worked by strings.

A zombie, straight out of Domnic's comic strip.

Rose shook her head to dispel the image. A leftover fragment of a dream, perhaps. But it stayed with her, itching in the back of her brain as she stepped out into the dreary hotel corridor and shut the door behind her.

Domnic's flat wasn't too hard to find. The roads were numbered rather than named, laid out in a grid system, and Rose was relieved to find she had only a few blocks to walk. She hadn't fancied trying to negotiate this world's public transport system without any cash and without the Doctor.

The lifts in Domnic's building were out, but fortunately he was only a few floors up. The bare concrete stairwell reminded Rose of the one in her own block, back home, but there was no graffiti. As if no one had anything to say.

She knocked on a flimsy wooden door for several minutes. She called through it, trying to reassure Domnic that she meant him no harm. She thought about kicking the door down, and would have done if she'd heard the slightest sound of movement from behind it.

He was probably at work. The call centre. She could have kicked herself for sleeping in, for leaving it too late.

What now?

She was trudging back to the hotel, deep in thought, when he leaped out at her from a table in front of a café. He'd been sitting, pretending to be engrossed in a newspaper in which the pictures seemed almost to outnumber the words.

'Domnic!' Rose squealed as he grabbed her arm and propelled her away.

He shushed her urgently. 'Just keep walking. They might be following you.'

Rose resisted the urge to look behind her. 'Who might be?'

'You've been to my flat. They've had cops patrolling all day, in plain clothes. I've been watching them. The same man, circling the block clockwise every three minutes. And there's someone in the flat across the road. I saw the sunlight flashing off an ocular lens.'

Rose did look now. 'I can't see anyone,' she said dubiously.

Domnic was setting a brisk pace, weaving expertly through the crowd, and Rose was struggling to keep up. She kept bumping into people. They reached a junction and abruptly he set off at a right angle. A moment later, he broke into a run and darted down an empty alleyway.

She caught up with him on the street at the far end. 'Look, I think it's OK,' she said. 'I don't think there's anyone…'

'They'd been in my flat,' said Domnic. 'I stayed last night with a friend and when I got home… They'd tried to put everything back as they found it, but I could tell. It was like everything was just… just a fraction out of place, you know? I came down the fire escape.'

'That's getting to be a habit.'

'Yeah, I'm sorry about that. I thought you were… well, I guess that was obvious. It must have been… The stress, the excitement, it must have made me a bit fantasy crazy. I realise now the chances of you being right there in that hotel room if you were… and, I mean, the police do lie to us, everyone knows that now, but the stories you were telling, they were *too* fantastic, unbelievable. They'd never…'

'OK, I get the point.'

'He was on again this morning,' said Domnic. 'Did you see him?'

'If you mean Hal Gryden…'

'Yeah,' he said excitedly. 'So you found him. What he was saying… I mean, this morning, I thought it was all over. You know, the police have my name – they must have forced it out of someone in the group

– and I can't go home, but I know now it won't be for long.'

'Why? What did he say?'

Domnic frowned. 'I thought you –'

'I only caught the last bit,' explained Rose.

Domnic was getting twitchy again, looking around them. His eyes narrowed and he took Rose by the arm again and pulled her down another alleyway. Paranoid, she thought, definitely paranoid. But maybe he had good reason. She was just passing through, but this was Domnic's life that had been turned upside down. She remembered how she had felt that first time, when the monsters had come to her workplace, her home. Like nothing made sense. At least she'd had the Doctor. Who did Domnic have?

Who else but her?

There was a scraping sound. As if someone had knocked against one of the bin lids behind them. They turned in unison, then looked at each other.

'There's no one there,' said Rose, trying to persuade herself as much as she was her companion.

Domnic nodded, but didn't look convinced. They hurried on, back into the crowds.

'You were gonna tell me about Gryden,' Rose prompted.

Domnic's voice was quieter, more subdued, than before. 'A year ago, he was nothing, just a rumour. I didn't think he existed. Now…'

'You really think he can change things.'

'I know he can. People listen to him, and now they know the truth – the real truth. And this morning… He's hinted about it before, but he's never actually come right out and said… A revolution, Rose. Hal Gryden says it's time for us to rise up and overthrow this police state. It's because we don't have a government, you see. There's no one to… to look at the way things are, to listen to us and to make a difference. So we have to form our own government! Gryden says it's time to repeal the anti-fiction laws, to demand our dreams and all the things they won't let us dream about. Yeah, those were his words… Rose, I think we're being…'

'I know.'

It was nothing she'd seen, nothing she'd heard. It was more a sense of dread, something lurking in the back of her brain. The sort of feeling she would normally have dismissed, but this time she couldn't. She was scanning the faces around her, looking for the one that would meet her eye.

And she gasped as she saw it, a half-block behind them, standing at the junction, its eyes black and vacant, its skin white and peeling.

And then the crowd closed around it and parted again, and it was gone.

Domnic must have seen it too, because suddenly they were both running.

They cut through a large department store, where everything was in plain black, white or grey packaging. She was beginning to doubt her own eyes. A zombie? How could there have been a zombie, right there on the pavement? With people walking past it as if it was nothing, as if they couldn't even see it?

Onto the street again, where they came to a stop because Domnic was out of breath.

'Did we shake her off?' he panted.

'"Her"?'

'I thought you saw her. The policewoman.'

'Um, yeah.' Now Rose really did feel stupid, seeing monsters where there had been none. But she'd been so sure. 'Yeah, I think we must've.'

To her surprise, Domnic placed his hands on her shoulders and stared earnestly into her eyes. 'I want you to know, Rose, that if we get caught, I won't tell them a thing. I'll say that I… I lied to you to make you help me. That in all the time I was with you I never heard you say anything that wasn't the whole truth…'

'Shut up, Domnic,' said Rose.

He recoiled, looking hurt. She had that dreadful feeling again. There was something behind her. To the left. To the right. But everywhere she turned, there were just ordinary people, most of them ignoring her but some now staring – at her clothes again? No, at the way she was acting. All twitchy.

The way Domnic had been acting last night. And now.

And it occurred to Rose that maybe this was how he felt all the time. As if there was something about this world... something she couldn't quite put her finger on. But she remembered what the Doctor had said about things beneath the surface, where most people couldn't see them. The feeling that, somewhere, there were monsters. If only she could work out where they were – and shake off the awful fear that, if she could see them, they could see her too.

Fantasy crazy.

And with that thought, Rose remembered something else she had heard. From Domnic, last night. About Hal Gryden. '*He opens our eyes...*'

'Static,' she gasped. 'That's what it's doing, isn't it? The programmes... somehow, they're making people *see*.'

'*... makes us look at the world in a different way.*'

Now it was her turn to take Domnic's arm and drag him along with her.

'Where are we going?' he cried.

'Find Jack and back to the TARDIS,' said Rose. 'And hope the Doctor finds us there. C'mon, it isn't safe out here.'

She wasn't running away, she told herself. She didn't run away. She was just... This made sense. This was more than she could handle. She needed...

'I… I can protect you, Rose.'

'You what?'

'It's up to me. I'm the man. I'm the hero.'

'Like hell! You ever done anything like this before?'

'Well… no, but…'

'Stick with me, then. I'll –' The words froze in her throat. She had caught the eye of a passer-by, just for an instant before he had looked down at his feet again.

And she *knew*.

'It's all of them,' she whispered.

'Wha – what do you…'

'They know, Domnic. Don't you see? They know that we know! All the people, everyone you can see, they're under the control of this… this… whatever it is that's controlling this world. Only we're free and they *know*.'

Domnic was nodding his head vigorously even as his eyes betrayed his lack of comprehension. 'You mean they're all informants. The police have put out a wanted bulletin, haven't they, and everyone knows our faces.'

And they were running down another alleyway, to the spot where it was crossed by another, and here they stopped because in all four directions there were roads and people – maintaining their fronts, the façades of their everyday lives, but Rose knew the truth. She knew the truth, and she knew they wouldn't allow her to expose it.

A shuffling sound. A woman cleared her throat and appeared through a tall wooden gate, weighed down by a pile of cardboard. Putting out the rubbish, or something more sinister? Rose wasn't sticking around to find out.

The first gate was locked. The second opened to her frantic jiggling of the latch and they burst into a tiny builder's yard. They were surrounded by piles of timber. Two doors led into the building proper, one directly ahead of them, the other at the top of a single flight of metal stairs. Rose's first thought was to take shelter inside, but she braked as some sense warned her of danger.

Was that someone at the window?

She'd only caught a glimpse out of the corner of her eye. A white-faced figure with hollow eyes and ragged clothing. When she tried to look at it directly, it disappeared and there was just the reflection of the sky in the dark glass.

The gate banged shut behind her, like a gunshot, making her jump. Rose knew there were more monsters behind it, sneaking up on her through the alleyways.

'Can you hear them?' she whispered.

'I can hear them,' Domnic confirmed, eyes wide with terror.

'This is it, Domnic. We're surrounded.'

He tried to pull away from her. 'I'll give myself up. I'll tell them it was my fault. You… you hide behind one of these piles of wood and maybe they won't…'

'This isn't one of your comics, Domnic, and you aren't my knight in shining armour. There's no way out of this for either of us.'

Rose grabbed a length of timber and wielded it like a club, her eyes fixed on the closed gate. The itch in her brain had turned into a full-blown buzz which seemed to drown out everything. The only semi-coherent thought she could form, somewhere in the back of her mind, was that the lighting was all wrong. Too bright. It was daytime, when night was the time for monsters.

Then the sun was swallowed by a bank of clouds and the yard fell into shadow.

And they came for her.

The gate flew open and there they were. Four of them, fighting to be the first to squeeze through the aperture. Rose turned, knowing what she would see before it happened: two more zombies appearing in the doorway of the building behind her. And another, emerging onto the staircase above her head, silent but for the shuffling of its feet.

Rose and Domnic stood back to back, surrounded. Domnic was whimpering. Rose hefted her makeshift weapon, ready to swing it at the first creature to come within range.

'I know what you're thinking,' she said with as much confidence as she could muster. 'I know what you want – but I'm not gonna scream or faint or fall out of my clothes, all right? So, if you want me… well, just bring it on!'

The zombies closed in.

# SEVEN

The Big White House was big. It was white. And it was a house.

At least, it had been a house once: a sprawling multi-winged mansion, built to a classical design, as distinct from the concrete towers around it as could be imagined. It even had its own grounds, to the Doctor's surprise, though they were small and paved over. He suspected that much of the house's land had been carved off for neighbouring developments – and what was left was cluttered with parked cars.

It couldn't really be described as a house any longer. It had had too many extensions grafted haphazardly onto it. The ugliest of them was a square block, five storeys high, which jutted up from the building's centre.

There was some peace to be gained here, though. The grounds were ringed by a wall, three metres high, which deadened much of the sound of the city – though the Doctor knew that that certainly wasn't its primary purpose.

A grey plaque on the outside of the wall had given the building no name, just a description: Home for the Cognitively Disconnected.

They'd been nodded through the gate by a guard as soon as he'd seen Waller's police bike and ill-fitting uniform; the Doctor had been reaching for his psychic paper, but had had no need of it. Anywhere else, he'd have been surprised by the lack of security. Here, though, he doubted anyone could conceive of anything so audacious as a jailbreak. Anyone outside of this building, anyway – until recently. Until Hal Gryden had begun the process of change.

The hallway was air-conditioned cool, painted in pastel colours. They were met by a young man of Oriental descent who wore a white coat over his grey jumpsuit. His eyes were red-rimmed, and the Doctor guessed he'd been working all night.

'Cal Tyko,' he introduced himself, 'duty nurse. I take it this is the prisoner?'

He glanced at the Doctor without really seeing him. When Waller corrected his misapprehension, repeating the Doctor's cover story, Tyko's features clouded. It was obvious he thought this a waste of his time.

'We won't get in your way,' the Doctor promised.

'I'm just looking for a few scare stories – you know, what happens to you when you lie, who comes for you, that kind of thing. Maybe a bit of technical jargon to make it sound plausible.'

Tyko raised an eyebrow. 'You need to make the truth sound "plausible"?'

'We've got competition these days, in case you hadn't noticed.'

Tyko sighed. 'You mean Gryden, don't you?'

'Dead right. What I want from this documentary is to restate a few basics but to back them up with evidence, make sure people believe us and not what they might see on the other side.' As he spoke, the Doctor darted around, making the shape of a TV screen with his fingers and looking at Tyko through them.

The nurse's attitude softened. 'I can give you an hour. I'm into overtime already, but the morning shift is short-staffed. And I've rounds to do – you'll have to keep up.'

'Glad to,' said the Doctor enthusiastically. 'I want to see everything.'

Tyko took them to a lift and up to the first floor of the tower block. 'I wish someone *could* do something about Gryden,' he lamented as he led them along a series of white-lit corridors. 'Every other patient we get in here these days has something to say about that fellow. And they're coming in thicker and faster. We don't have the beds. We've been sending the minor cases out to private clinics. I tell you, if I could get my hands on him…'

'Yeah,' said the Doctor mildly, 'but "if" is a dangerous word.'

Nurse Tyko nodded, looking a bit shamefaced.

They came to a whitewashed metal door. Tyko opened a hatch in it to reveal a barred window. Through this the Doctor could see a tiny dorm with another barred window at its far side. It was furnished with a bed, a chest of drawers and the ubiquitous flat TV screen taking up fully half of one wall. The TV was on, but the sound was turned down, the subtitles on. A young woman lay on the bed, wearing a plain white nightgown. She was painfully thin.

'Morning, Su,' said Tyko. 'You had your breakfast?'

'I've been a good girl, Mr Tyko. I ate it all up, I did.'

'You know we can check, don't you? Show me the plate.'

The woman gave him a resentful look, then forced herself into a sitting position, picked up an empty plate from the floor and tilted it towards him.

'Very good, Su. The orderlies will collect it soon. Do you need a pill this morning?'

Su shook her head. Tyko nodded, satisfied, and closed the hatch.

'I think we're getting somewhere with Su,' he said as they strolled on. 'Of course, the orderlies will check under the bed and behind the drawers, but it's been a few weeks since she lied to us, and she's certainly getting stronger. Silly girl, she wanted to look like the women she saw on Static. Her friends told her that imaginary food tasted as good as the real thing and helped you lose weight. When she first came in, she could hardly stand by herself.'

'She can't tell fantasy from reality, is that it?'

'Who can?' said Tyko. 'This next fellow, he couldn't accept that his grandma had passed away. He kept her in his flat for six months. He imagined she was talking to him. It was only when she persuaded him to take her out shopping…'

'Ah,' said the Doctor.

There were more after that – many more, filling dozens of rooms and no doubt many more above them. People who had been committed for fraud or assault or just for eccentricity, all with one thing in common. They had acted as they had, or so they claimed, because they had believed in something unreal: voices in their heads, whispers behind their backs or just dreams of bettering themselves.

Tyko addressed each of them with unstinting politeness, dispensing encouragement and – guided by a data pad – pills in varying strengths and dosages. Sometimes he made a note on the pad before they moved on. The Doctor strode alongside him, ever cheerful, hands clasped behind his back, asking interested questions. Waller said nothing, a brooding presence in her black police helmet. Only when Tyko commented that the number of admissions for violent crimes had increased sharply in recent months did she grumble something to herself.

Back on the ground floor, the Doctor spotted signs for two operating theatres. Tyko was adamant that they were off-limits. A sterile environment, he said – and any further discussion was forestalled by the bleeping of his pager.

The nurse unclipped the small white device from his belt, read a message on its screen and scowled. 'It appears I won't be home on time today after all,' he said. 'They've just brought us another guest.'

Arno Finch didn't resist as he was unloaded from the back of a police transport vehicle. It was only when he saw where he was that he began to struggle. He was outnumbered, though, and his hands were still cuffed.

Four cops carried him into the Big White House, four more following with guns drawn. Nurse Tyko made a token attempt to direct them, but they knew where they were going.

'Strictly speaking, there should be a doctor handling this,' Tyko confided to the Doctor and

Waller as they hurried after the new arrivals, 'but we're stretched to the limit.'

'And you can't take on more staff?' the Doctor ventured.

'No,' said Tyko and Waller in unison.

'Cos that's not the way things are. OK.'

He recognised some of the officers from the scene of Finch's crime. They'd raced past him into the office block as he and Waller had left it. Waller hadn't even acknowledged them, marching stiffly up to her bike, keen to move on. Of course, the Doctor never liked to stick around for the mopping up either.

Tyko showed them into a small, windowless room with a desk, two chairs and a computer, and shut them in. Two walls were covered in TV screens. Each showed the inside of an inmate's room – the cameras seemed to be hidden behind their own TVs – apart from the biggest, most central screen, on which a featureless cell with white padded walls was displayed. A moment passed, then the door of this cell flew open.

Arno Finch was hurled to the floor, unable to use his hands to break his fall. Four cops took a limb each and pinned him down as Tyko came in, holding a hypodermic needle filled with a clear liquid. The nurse stooped beside Finch, muttered something soothing to him, and slid the needle into his neck.

'What's he doing?' asked the Doctor.

'Shutting down the right hemisphere of the brain,' said Waller stiffly. 'That's the subconscious side, the side that deals with fiction.'

'Yeah, I know what it does.'

Tyko straightened and nodded to the escorting officers before leaving the room. One of the cops directed two bursts of a solvent spray at Finch's bound wrists, then hurried out with his colleagues. The door closed again and the Doctor could hear the clunks of locks being engaged.

'They got here quick, don't you think?' he remarked to Waller.

'Maybe there was a wagon in the area.'

'Not what I meant. Your lot must have brought Finch straight here. No questioning, no trial, nothing.'

'No need,' said Waller. 'He's a fiction geek. It's up to the doctors to decide his treatment. You'll see.'

Cal Tyko had appeared in the white cell again, without the door opening. A hologram, the Doctor deduced, probably operated from a nearby control booth. It gave off a tell-tale fizz as it stood beside Finch, who was lying where he'd fallen, blubbering to himself. Tyko spoke to him in gentle tones, assuring him that he was safe, that the doctors would protect him from the nightmares and that if he could just answer a few simple questions and provide his credit number then everyone would be happy.

Finch, his hands free now, tried to lever himself into

a sitting position. He gave up and burst into a renewed flood of tears when he realised that the left side of his body was paralysed.

'It's OK,' Tyko reassured him. 'This is just a temporary side effect of your medicine, that's all.'

The Doctor glanced at Waller. 'You must be hot in that helmet.'

'I'm fine.'

'Must be stuffy,' he said. When she didn't answer, he persisted, 'Just wondered what it's for, that's all. You don't reckon you need protecting in here? Didn't think so. And it can't be to intimidate the bad guys, cos that'd imply you want them to use their right hemispheres. You know, to imagine what's behind the black visor.'

'They don't have to imagine,' said Waller sharply. 'They can see I'm a police officer. That's all anyone needs to know.'

On the screen, the holographic Tyko was asking Finch about his childhood. The answers came resentfully and were slurred as Finch struggled to speak through one side of his mouth. Tyko responded to each one with a weary tick on his data pad.

'OK,' said the Doctor. 'My fault. I know you didn't want to come here. I thought maybe you had something to hide.'

There was a long silence. The Doctor stood, smiling innocently.

He didn't expect Waller to lie, of course. Which left her with only one choice.

She took off the helmet.

They both stared fixedly at the screen for a few seconds. Then the Doctor risked a sidelong glance.

Waller was a dark-skinned woman, approaching middle age, with shaved greying hair and a misshapen nose that had obviously been broken a time or two. She was standing almost to attention, obstinately avoiding the Doctor's eye.

'Nope,' he said. 'Don't see anything wrong there. Two eyes, two ears, the right number of noses, all in the right places. No hideous scarring. Must be the other thing, then.' Waller didn't take the bait, so the Doctor asked a question of his own. 'When were you here?'

'A lifetime ago,' she confessed grudgingly.

'But you're still afraid they'll recognise you. Was Tyko here then?'

'No. It can happen to anyone, you know.'

'I'll bet.'

'I was a teenager. You know what it's like. No matter what they tell you, you can never quite resist the dreams. The dreams feel good. Until you get older. Until it goes bad for the first time.'

'How long did they keep you in?'

'Sixteen months,' said Waller bitterly. 'Sixteen months out of my life, and the worst thing is I've no one to blame but myself. No one can say they weren't warned. No one can say they haven't seen.'

'But they let you go.'

'I was one of the lucky ones. They taught me to repress the images. I couldn't do my job otherwise. It means everything to me, Doctor. When I'm out on the streets, on my bike, everything is clear. Everything is black and white. I know the procedures. I can throw myself into the work because it's real, because it's now, because I enjoy it – and because, while I'm doing it, it's as if the ghosts aren't there for a while.'

Tyko had finished his questioning of Finch. He explained to him that he'd be kept in the padded cell a while longer, under observation, to make sure he wasn't a danger to himself. Then, as soon as a room became free, he would be moved to it. Finch nodded, accepting his fate without argument. He dragged himself into a corner, hampered by a useless arm and leg, and moped there.

'You ever see Static?' asked the Doctor.

'No,' said Waller. 'Doctor… this documentary of yours. I can't be a part of it. It's best that way. After we leave here, I can't see you again.'

It was a long time before either of them said another word.

'Y'see,' said the Doctor, 'I get that fiction is dangerous.

Took me a while, but I get it now. I even understand how, but not why.'

Tyko slid a plastic card through a reader beside the main entrance door – clocking off, the Doctor surmised – and led his visitors out into the grounds. 'We don't ask that question,' he said.

'You don't ask much at all.'

'We don't like to imagine the answers.'

'But you know this isn't right. You haven't forgotten your history. You know the human race dreamed once, or you'd never have got this far.'

'True,' said Waller, 'but look what it cost them. Our ancestors flirted with madness. They let their criminals run rampant, accepted that their leaders would always lie to them, fought wars over things they couldn't see. Billions of them suffered and died to give us what we have now.'

'And what is that, exactly?'

'A stable and workable society. A reality in which we can all live, in which we don't *have* to dream any more.'

'No, I'm not having that.' The Doctor shook his head stubbornly. 'I'd say it was hysteria, but I don't see any other symptoms… Kids aren't affected, you said?'

'There have been no extreme cases under the age of thirteen,' said Tyko.

'Though it's best they learn to resist fiction from

the start,' said Waller, 'get them into the habit.'

'You're living in fear,' opined the Doctor. 'You're living in fear, and you're too... too mired in dogma to do anything about it.'

Tyko shrugged. 'It's the way things are. We've good reason to be afraid of the big bad wolf.'

'Oops,' said the Doctor, 'now you're using a metaphor.'

Tyko shot him a glare, but then forced a smile. 'You're right again, of course. Now, if you'll excuse me, both of you, I have another shift in a few hours.'

They had reached his car – though how Tyko could tell it from all the other grey vehicles was a mystery. He climbed into the driver's seat and started the engine.

'I have to go too,' said Waller, stifling a yawn. She put her helmet back on and made for her bike. 'Can I drop you somewhere?'

The Doctor had stayed out longer than he'd meant to. Rose and Captain Jack would have woken by now and found him gone.

'I'm staying at a hotel,' he said, 'just round the corner from where we met.'

Waller grimaced apologetically. 'It's a bit out of my way.'

'I'll blag a lift off someone. It's no trouble.' He just hoped his companions hadn't done anything unwise. They didn't know what he now knew.

Waller nodded and kicked her bike into gear. As it rose on its jets, she said she hoped the Doctor's research had been fruitful. He assured her that it had. She hesitated.

'Our world,' she said. 'Its name. I did hear something. It was a long time ago. Some of the girls at school, they said it was called – I mean, it used to be called – Journey's End. As if this was where we came to put our struggles behind us.'

The Doctor flashed her a grateful smile.

Waller rode to the gate, her bike's engines whining, and he followed on foot, waving to the guard as he passed him.

The street outside the Big White House was almost empty. As if everyone – drivers and pedestrians alike – avoided this block when they could.

Standing alone, the Doctor let his façade slip for a moment. He watched Waller's bike receding into the distance, until it turned onto a road clogged with traffic and was gone. He remembered all she had said to him and he felt a stab of remorse. He empathised with her a great deal more than she could ever realise.

But he also knew what he had to do – and he knew that, like it or not, Inspector Waller would be one of the first casualties.

# EIGHT

Jack had waited a long time under the bridge for Hal Gryden to return. Long enough to fear he had been forgotten, or that the old man had been playing some kind of joke on him all along; worse still, that maybe whatever he had planned had backfired.

'We can't rely on money,' Gryden had explained. 'I have credits, millions of them, but I don't dare access my accounts except in an emergency. The police are always watching.' Which left him with few options – and fewer legal ones – if he was to do what he had said he would.

At last, however, Jack heard a rustling sound. He pulled back into the shadows, just in case, but it was Gryden who emerged from the bushes further down the river bank. He was carrying a crumpled white plastic bag, which turned out to contain a grey jumpsuit. The price tag was still attached to it, though

Gryden confessed with a wink that he knew how to disable the store's security chip.

Jack changed quickly and stuffed his own clothes into the bag, hiding it in the bushes in case he got the chance to come back for it.

'Time we moved on, Cap'n,' said Gryden. 'We should be less conspicuous now. I've a studio a few blocks from here. We'll put you on air and you can tell your stories to the world. Your enthusiasm is just what we need to see.'

Jack couldn't get over the change in him. He was standing taller and his voice was deeper and more confident. He seemed like a new man.

Gryden led the way up a flight of corroded iron steps half buried by the undergrowth into a gloomy alleyway behind a residential building. They emerged onto a street and had soon become part of the constant crowd.

'You must have quite an operation,' Jack remarked, keeping his voice low in case a passer-by should overhear. 'I mean, if everything I've heard is true. How many programmes do you make?'

'As many as we can,' said Gryden.

'It can't be easy.'

'It wasn't. In the beginning, there were only a few of us. We started by publishing an underground magazine. Distribution was our main problem – but the more people we reached, the more came on board to help us and the more we could achieve. Now we can reach the whole world. Oh, I know we can't compete with the official channels technically – we've so little experience, because no one has done anything like this before. And yes, our effects are primitive and our sets sometimes wobble. No one really minds. It's the stories they want to see.'

'What about the police? I told a few stories in a few pubs and they were right on to me. How do your actors and presenters cope? Aren't they recognised?'

'Did you recognise me in that shop doorway?'

'Well, actually,' confessed Jack, 'I've never seen Static.'

Gryden shot him a bemused look, as if he didn't quite believe him. 'Hiding is easier than you think,' he said, 'if you know what you're doing. We use make-up and costumes to change how our on-screen personalities look. We provide rooms in our studios so they don't have to go out in public any more than necessary. But our biggest ally is the fact that people don't look. They're so busy concentrating on their own sad lives, they don't want to think about what else there might be.'

'Yeah, well,' said Jack, 'we'll soon change that.'

'Anyway,' said Gryden with a smirk, 'I use a double. The Hal Gryden you see on TV, that's not me, Cap'n, that's an actor.'

Jack frowned. 'So you're lying to them too? To your public?'

'Why not?' Gryden clapped him cheerfully on the back. 'Isn't that what this is all about, the freedom to tell as many lies as we want?'

'Fair point.'

'Do you know what this world is called?' asked Gryden. 'Oh, I don't mean Colony World 4378-blah-blah, that's just a designation, a number on a list. I mean its *name*, the one the space pioneers gave it. This world is called Oneiros. Do you like it?'

'Catchy,' said Jack.

'It's Greek,' said Gryden, 'from their ancient mythology. The Oneiroi were the carriers of dreams. That's what this ball of rock meant to our ancestors. They brought their dreams here, they left them to us – and they didn't do that so we could watch them die.'

They made their way to a run-down sector of town where the buildings were crumbling and many had been abandoned. Several boasted signs that promised forthcoming redevelopment. In the meantime, though, the windows were boarded up, gravel from the roadway speckled the pavements and litter had been left to clog the drains. A street light flashed on and off spasmodically, even in daylight, and the only info-screen in view was broken.

The traffic was still regular, though: drivers looking

for short cuts or just a respite from the congestion of the main streets. And people still passed by on foot, albeit in small clusters of mostly young men, drifting without apparent aim.

No one spared them a glance as they slipped around the side of an old warehouse building. Gryden had been right about that much.

There was a row of small, semicircular windows at ground level. On one of them, the boarding had come loose and Gryden pulled it back like a hatchway to reveal a dark space behind. He wriggled through the hole and dropped out of sight. Jack followed eagerly, without waiting for an invite.

Inside, the warehouse was dark and dusty. The window through which they had entered was above their heads now, and the only light came from this or crept in around the boards of the other windows. The light picked out silver cobwebs in the ceiling joists. Bulky shapes lurked around them, and as Jack's eyes adjusted he saw that they were wooden crates: hundreds of them, stacked haphazardly.

There were sheets and moth-eaten blankets strewn about, as if somebody had been sleeping down here. Jack's foot touched an empty bottle.

And there was a figure – its face chalk white, its red lips pulled back into a sinister sneer. One of Gryden's staff? But then why hadn't he introduced himself? Why lurk in the shadows, so silent and still?

He was standing at Gryden's shoulder and Jack wasn't sure if the old man had seen him. His first instinct was to push Gryden aside, to protect him. But he realised now that the figure wasn't a man at all, just a crude effigy. A punching bag, with a clown's face on it. Jack gave it a shove, and it wobbled and returned to an upright position. The clown's grin appeared to be mocking him.

Many of the crates had been burst open and Jack dropped to his haunches to examine some of the contents.

They were toys. Brightly coloured pots of putty with intelligent memory, thought-controlled Frisbees, model spaceships.

'The last thing they took from us,' said Gryden. 'According to the history books, there was a furious debate. Some people thought our children, at least, should be able to enjoy their dreams while they could – but the majority were afraid we were teaching them bad habits. And there were health and safety issues to do with exposing workers to dangerous ideas. In the end, the toys were banned but not burned like the storybooks had been. Then the government was disbanded.'

'And the toys were all sealed up and forgotten,' surmised Jack, 'left here to rot.' Except that, at some point, someone had obviously unearthed and explored this treasure trove. Good on them.

A board game had been laid out in the dust, apparently abandoned in mid-session, its pieces and cards sent flying by escaping feet. Jack found the box and squinted at it in the gloom: 'NIGHTMARES. A game of life, where the object is to succeed without going fantasy crazy. Can you find a flat and a good job before your dreams catch up with you? Not suitable for ages 11+'.

He flung the box aside and it landed by chance in an open crate packed with yellow rubber ducks. The silence was shattered as six of the birds took flight, flapping and quacking about their heads. It took them a nerve-jangling minute to recapture and deactivate them all.

Gryden led the way deeper into the warehouse, deeper into the darkness, until they found a hydraulic platform big enough to carry two cars. It was stuck at shoulder height, leaving a rectangular hole in the ceiling. A few crates had been arranged around the platform like steps, allowing them to clamber onto it. From here, they could haul themselves up onto the ground floor of the building.

As Jack got to his feet, he noted that the dust around him lay thick, as if nobody had been this way in years. There were more crates, but these too were undisturbed. He knew there were more floors above them, but he'd expected some sign of habitation by now. Still, if this was only a backup studio, maybe

Gryden had established it a while ago and hadn't had cause to use it before now.

The old man certainly didn't seem familiar with his surroundings; not as he had been below. He stumbled into crate after crate, finding a path through by touch alone. 'There'll be a staircase along here somewhere,' he muttered – but suddenly he didn't sound so sure.

And then there were footsteps and shouting and light – blue light – and it was too late. The police had found them.

They'd come in through the warehouse's main doors. Presumably they had some kind of override code for the locks. Jack didn't know if he and Gryden had been followed, or if someone had noticed and reported them after all. It hardly mattered. All they could do, either way, was run.

They turned back the way they'd come, hoping the police didn't know about their secret entrance. They were thwarted by the sight of black uniforms already swarming onto the hydraulic platform below them, guns snapping up to take aim. They leaped back as blue energy balls thudded into the ceiling, dislodging a shower of dust.

The lightshow pinpointed their location for the other cops and they closed in. Someone shouted that they were surrounded, that the only way out of this was to show themselves with their hands up. She was probably right.

Gryden was starting to panic, shaking and gasping for breath.

Jack took him firmly by the shoulders. 'The studio. If we're gonna go down, we'll do it live on TV. We can show everyone what's really going on on this world.'

Gryden nodded dumbly.

They played cat and mouse through the crates with their pursuers, using the cover to their best advantage, and Jack soon estimated that they'd broken through the police cordon. The cops, fortunately, were paying most attention to the exits, so the stairs, when they finally came into view, were unguarded.

But that was where their luck let them down. A warning cry was raised in a gruff voice and suddenly the air was thick with blaster fire. Gryden yelped as he was hit in the side and Jack had to practically carry him into the enclosed stairwell. They had cover here, but it wouldn't last. They climbed as fast as they could, but Gryden was short of breath, clutching his bruise and gritting his teeth, and Jack was painfully aware of the ringing of booted footsteps gaining on them from below.

And of another sound. A whirring of motors.

'A lift! Why the hell didn't you tell me there was a lift?'

'Needs a key card,' Gryden gasped. 'We couldn't have used it.'

'But the cops can. They're behind us, and now they're ahead of us too.'

'I… I think I need… I really need to lie down, Cap'n. Just for a minute. That shot… I was lucky. They missed the main nerve clusters, but… I can't feel my arm.'

Jack made a decision. He set off down the stairs again, to Gryden's visible alarm. At the nearest turn, he waited with his back to the wall, listening, counting down under his breath.

The first cop to appear was still taking in the sight of Gryden, slumped on the stairs above him, when Jack jumped him. There was a brief struggle, during which the cop's gun went off three times and Gryden tried to scramble for cover. But Jack managed to wrest the weapon from his opponent's hand. He took a step back and fired.

He'd aimed over the cop's head; he hadn't had time to check that the gun wasn't set to kill. The shot still had the desired effect. The cop disappeared back round the corner and Jack sent three more bolts thudding into the wall after him for good measure. Then he returned to Gryden, bundled him to his feet and dragged him along, onwards and upwards.

The lift had stopped moving a few floors above them.

'How much further?' asked Jack. 'Where's the studio?'

'F-fourth floor,' Gryden mumbled.

Another flight and a half. Jack wasn't sure he could make it, not with his companion's near-dead weight slowing him down. He couldn't leave him behind, though.

Another turn of the stairs and he could see it: the doorway onto the fourth floor. But boots were clattering down from above, and the boots behind were nearer now too, though they seemed to be advancing more warily than before.

Circles of light played across the wall ahead. Flashlight beams. The police above were closer to the doorway; they would reach it before he and Gryden could. He looked at his gun. It was no more advanced than many he'd seen back home. It was a simple matter to overload its power pack: a remarkably common design flaw, and one that had its uses.

He hurled the weapon up the stairs, angling it so that it bounced into view of the cops on the next flight. He shouted to Gryden to get down, but belied his words by continuing to pull him along. By the time the cops realised that the gun *wasn't* about to explode, he and Gryden had beaten them to the doorway.

Jack thought about leaving the gun – he couldn't retrieve it without sticking his head into the line of fire. It was all he had, though. It might only hold the cops off for a few more seconds, but each one would count. He dived for the weapon and scooped it up, coming away with the brief impression of a stairwell crowded with black uniforms, too surprised to react to his brief appearance, still picking themselves up after their bomb scare.

Jack felt a surge of elation as he raced through the doorway, into…

… emptiness. No studio, no crates – just space, stretching out before him.

He kept going, because he couldn't quite believe it. There had to be a secret room or a lift. Just something, somewhere, because if there wasn't…

If there wasn't…

He came to a helpless stop in the centre of the floor. He heard shuffling on the stairwell and automatically sent three shots in that direction to discourage pursuit, though there seemed little point now. He could see right through to the boarded-up windows on all four sides of the building, and Gryden had dropped to his knees and was holding on to Jack's legs and giggling hysterically.

'Where is it?' asked Jack urgently, though he was sure he knew the answer by now. 'You said there was a studio here. Where is it?'

'It's here,' sniggered the tramp. 'It's all around us. Can't you see? There are the lights up there, and the cameras standing there, there and there. We're on air. The whole world is watching us, and you'll tell them, won't you, Cap'n? You'll tell them how things are, and they'll never be able to ignore us again because we'll be famous, won't we? We'll be famous!'

Jack laid down the gun with a sigh and kicked it away from him.

The police approached with caution, suspecting a trap, but still they approached. They formed a circle of raised guns around the two fugitives.

Captain Jack put up his hands. The man who had called himself Hal Gryden was no longer laughing.

As four officers came for them and pulled them apart from each other, the tramp began to panic again.

'Cap'n, don't let them do this! Why are you just standing there? You said it'd be OK. You said if I came with you, you could fix everything.'

Jack avoided his eye, staring stubbornly at the ground. He felt disgusted, and he couldn't face his betrayer, didn't want to tell him what he was thinking, because he knew it wasn't really the old man's fault. He was ill. So Jack could only feel disgust with himself, for not seeing it in time.

'You have the right to remain silent,' growled a voice in his ear. 'Anything you do say had better be the truth, or you're for it!'

They were spray-cuffed and marched to the stairs, Jack maintaining a resigned silence as the tramp babbled in fear: 'Listen to me, you've got the wrong man, it's not my fault. It was this man… This man, he told me he was a captain of a spaceship, and I thought… I could see he was fantasy crazy, but he made me come with him, he made me steal for him. He had a gun and he wouldn't let me go. He said he was going to spread fiction to the whole world, but I didn't listen to his stories, I didn't. You can't take me to the Big White House, I've done nothing wrong. I know what they do to you there, and I can't face that. I'd rather die, do you hear me? I'd rather die, and that's the truth!'

# NINE

**D**omnic had never met a girl like Rose Tyler. In his job he spoke to dozens of women every day, and most of them were the same: self-absorbed, uninterested. His co-workers went straight from the office to a club, where they stood, not talking, swaying in time to an overbearing drumbeat. The music had no melody, no lyrics. Its only purpose was to drown out reality, when Domnic knew that music could do so much more.

He couldn't see the world their way and they ridiculed him for that. They called him a geek, and probably worse behind his back. Some of them – and he could see this in their eyes when he approached them, hear it in the hush that so often presaged his appearance – were scared of him, scared that one day he might freak out.

When he'd joined the reading group, he had hoped to

find a soul mate, someone who shared his perspective.

At first, there had been Manda. Mad Mand, they had called her. She had never had the discipline to write her ideas down, but when the mood struck her she would take centre stage with a series of ad hoc and increasingly extravagant tales, losing herself so deeply in the fiction that her recitals left Domnic breathless.

He had found his tongue tied whenever she had spoken to him. She just seemed to know what he was still trying to learn. She seemed to get it.

But gradually her stories had lost any grounding in reality. They'd become longer and more rambling, lacking in structure – aimless flights of fantasy that made sense to no one but herself. And now, when the others had called her 'mad', it had been with concern in their voices rather than admiration.

Mad Mand had smashed up a restaurant one day. She had threatened the customers with a table leg. The staff had tried to restrain her, but they'd said on the news channels later that she'd had the strength of ten. In the end, in desperation, the chef had reached for a knife.

Manda had still been laughing, in her baritone boom, as she was carried into the ambulance. She had died in a traffic jam, halfway to the hospital.

Domnic had shunned the reading group for a month. It had taken him that long to come to terms with what had happened. The media had seized on the incident, citing it as an example of the danger of fiction, but that wasn't right. It had been the danger that had seduced Manda to start with. She hadn't been interested in the stories for their own sake, just in the thrill of dicing with insanity. If fiction hadn't killed her, she would have found something else to do the job.

At least, that was how Domnic rationalised it to himself.

Later, thanks to the news channels, they had found out a lot about Mad Mand – about her parents and a succession of bad boyfriends. They had come to see why it was that she had been so scared of reality.

Domnic, in the meantime, had returned to the group to find Nat. Poor, sweet Nat. Seventeen years old and so nervous, approaching each new story with trepidation, always feeling that she was doing something terribly wrong. Domnic had had to talk her out of leaving a few times. She'd stayed because she said a love story made her feel sort of liquid inside. She had written one once and had wept as she read it out loud. She hadn't read Domnic's stories, because she said they were too violent. She had been scared of ending up like Manda.

When she and Domnic had kissed, that one time, he hadn't been sure if she had been kissing him or some idealised image of the male romantic hero.

The doctors had Nat now. They would make her feel like a criminal, when she had done no harm to anybody. Even if she was released from the Big White House, he knew he'd never see her again.

And then there was Rose, and she'd been everything Domnic had ever wanted or wanted to be: bright, enthusiastic, confident. She had thrown herself into fiction in a way that Nat would never have dared, taking the good but leaving the bad, letting it energise her but not control her. Unlike Mad Mand, she had still known what was real. She had balanced both worlds, and made it look easy. Until now.

Until, to Domnic's horror and dismay, Rose Tyler had fallen to pieces before his eyes. Until she had started to swing a plank of wood at thin air and to shout at nothing. And she had that wild, frightened look in her eyes as they flicked from side to side, looking for imaginary terrors everywhere.

She was fantasy crazy. The news channels had been right all along. And all those other women… For the first time, Domnic really understood what it was they had been so scared of.

He tried to tell Rose there was nothing there, that the yard was empty, but she wasn't listening. He took her by the arm and made to guide her away, but she shrugged him off. Then she whirled round and her face lit up with relief. And she cried out a single word: 'Doctor!'

She made for the metal staircase behind them, coming back for Domnic when she realised he was watching, dumbfounded. She took his hand and dragged him up the stairs after her, but came up short as if there was something in their path. 'No,' she warned, 'don't touch it!' And she stared around with those wild eyes again.

The stairs bent back on themselves, and Rose climbed onto the handrail and jumped for the one above. She caught it and pulled herself nimbly up and over. She turned to reach for Domnic and cried his name in alarm as she saw that he had taken the easy way round. Her face clouded with confusion, just for a moment.

'OK, Doctor,' she called, 'we're coming!'

She shouldered open the door into the building. They barged through a small, untidy storeroom and into an office area, where a prim-looking woman leaped up from her desk and demanded to know who they were. 'No time to explain,' said Rose, 'just get out of here. Get everyone out! There are zombies behind us!' And then she was gone, leaving Domnic to mutter an embarrassed apology as he hurried after her.

He caught up with her downstairs, in a short passageway from which several doors led, presumably into more offices.

She clutched at him in desperation. 'Where'd he go?

Did you see where he went?'

'Who?'

'The Doctor!'

'I didn't see any doctor.'

'How d'you think we got out of there? He was up on the stairs. He used the sonic screwdriver, and he… I don't know, he confused the zombies or something.'

'I didn't see any… zombies.' Zombies?

'You been walking around with your eyes shut?'

'I mean there *were* no zombies. You imagined them.' And it was all his fault. His comic strip. He'd planted those images in Rose's mind.

She looked incredulous. 'You heard them. You said.'

'I heard the cops. I thought they were following us. But it was fiction, Rose.' He was shaking her, as if he could shake her back to reality. 'Don't you see? There were no cops. There are no zombies, no doctor…'

He thought he'd been getting through to her, but now she broke away from him.

'The Doctor isn't fiction. What are you doing? Why're you trying to confuse me? I can't think straight.'

'OK,' said Domnic, 'OK, you're under treatment, I get it. So tell me where. Tell me where this doctor's practice is and we'll go there. We'll get help.'

'I don't know where,' insisted Rose. 'He was here, but he's gone.'

'He wasn't here. I didn't see him.'

'The TARDIS. I can show you his TARDIS. It's out in the jungle. C'mon, you'll believe me then. The TARDIS, it's the Doctor's ship.'

'*His* ship? Then who was that "Captain Jack" guy?'

'The Doctor travels in time. He fights monsters. There were these shop-window dummies that were alive and they were going to kill me, and the Doctor was there, and we've been to the past and the future and...'

'Listen to yourself, Rose. Does this sound right? Does it sound like fact?' Had he been like this last night? Was this how he had seemed to her? He'd always told himself he could handle it, but now...

'They were real, Domnic. I could smell them, like rotting fruit. I even felt a chill from the one on the stairs as I climbed past it.'

'Forget about the zombies, Rose. I... I've seen this sort of thing on TV. They give you advice. They say you should... You should focus on something real, something you believe in.'

'The Doctor.'

'Not him. Your home. Your family. Just think about them, nothing else. Or... or something like... that table over there. That table's real, Rose. You can see it, I can see it. Concentrate on the table.'

'Home!' said Rose. She was rummaging in her pockets. 'I can phone home. I can talk to Mum. She'll know. She'll tell you. And she's met the Doctor. I can prove it to you. I can prove he's real.'

'What on earth *is* that?' asked Domnic as Rose produced a boxy device, not dissimilar to a TV remote control.

'It's my mobile. My... er, vidphone. Without the "vid".'

'It's the size of a brick!'

'Wait till you see what it can do.'

She pressed a couple of keys, then held the phone up so that they could both hear the ring tone on the other end of the line. It repeated eight times before it was cut off by a crackle and a tired, husky, irritable voice: *'Yeah?'*

'Mum, it's me.'

A long silence.

*'Rose? Rose, what're you... Where are you? D'you know what time it is?'*

Rose was grinning, almost in tears. 'Mum, I don't know what *day* it is there.'

*'Did he bring you home? Tell me he's brought you home.'*

'Mum, listen...'

*'Though if he did, I s'pose I'd be the last to know. Cardiff, Rose. It's only up the motorway. You could've given me a call.'*

'I can give you a call from anywhere. From here.'

*'I saw Mickey. What've you done to that poor boy, Rose? I mean, I mightn't have had much time for him before, but all he's been through for you...'*

'I know. Mum…'

The grin had frozen into a grimace. Rose pressed the phone to her ear so that Domnic could no longer hear the other side of her conversation. For the next minute or so she just listened impatiently and occasionally tried to break in.

At last, she said, 'It's just… I needed to hear your voice… No, Mum, there's nothing wrong… Look, I've gotta go… Yeah, yeah, soon, I promise. Bye, Mum.'

And she cut off the connection and stared at the phone glassy-eyed.

Domnic felt he ought to say something, but the more time passed the harder it got. Finally, clumsily, he asked, 'This Mickey… is he your boyfriend?'

'Not any more,' sighed Rose. She took a deep, steadying breath. 'I know what's real now, Domnic. Mum's real. Mickey's real. The zombies – they weren't real. I can see that now, but at the time…'

'And this doctor?'

'The realest thing I've ever known. And you're right, we've gotta find him – but he's not at some practice and I'm not going running back to the TARDIS. The hotel! We should go back to the hotel.'

Domnic felt a tingle in his spine as they crossed the hotel lobby. They ran into a cleaner outside the lifts and he half expected him to raise the alarm, but he passed them by without a glance. Last night, this building had been alive with shadows and threats, but they had been fiction. Today, the same corridors, the same rooms, were dingy and mundane.

'You know, this world had a name once,' he said.

'Yeah?'

'It was called Discovery – because that's what it was to the pioneers. Something new, something special. I'd love to have lived back then, when life was an adventure. Now it's just a way of getting from birth to death.'

In Rose's room they found a note she had written to the Doctor, untouched. There was no sign that he'd been here.

'What if they got to him too?' she asked worriedly. 'What if they managed to drive *him* crazy? I'm serious, Domnic. Whatever's behind this... If anyone's gonna find the monsters, it's him, and if they've caught him...'

'Something real, Rose,' urged Domnic. 'Focus!'

'The Doctor's real,' she muttered to herself fiercely.

He'd turned on the TV and was fiddling with the tuning controls again.

'D'you think that's a good idea?' asked Rose.

'Hal Gryden will know what to do,' said Domnic. 'He'll make things clearer.'

'... *Hal Gryden*...' said the TV, like an echo.

'Is that it?' asked Rose. 'Is that Static?'

'I don't think…' Domnic was looking at a familiar newsreader and a channel ident that read '8 News'. But he hadn't imagined what he had just heard… had he?

*– drama plays in which the police are portrayed as inflexible, corrupt monsters with a hidden agenda. The cumulative effect of exposure to such fiction –*

He grabbed the remote control and flicked through the official channels.

'*– man is dangerous. His description is unknown –*'

'*– changes his appearance –*'

'*– Gryden –*'

This couldn't be happening. His heart was beating against his chest.

'*– station is a huge undertaking and somebody must know –*'

'*– must be apprehended for all our –*'

'*– Hal –*'

'*– outbreaks of violence, ranging from –*'

'*– urge our viewers not to listen to this man's lies –*'

'What's going on?' asked Rose.

Domnic had to swallow before he could answer. He couldn't believe it. He could hardly find the words. 'He's done it. He… he's made the news. Hal Gryden's made the news!'

'So? I thought everyone knew about him already.'

'Yeah, of course… of course. But don't you see? It's

official now. All these years, the police and the media have been ignoring him, pretending that Static didn't exist, when everyone knew... Well, look now, Rose. Look what's happening. Hal Gryden is on every single channel.'

Rose was just beginning to understand. She came to kneel beside Domnic, hypnotised as he was by the TV screen.

'I get it. They thought he'd go away if they didn't tell anyone about him.'

'But it didn't work. Word spread anyway, and he only got stronger.'

'So now they can't ignore him any more.'

'They've brought him out into the open. They've made him real.'

'So they can fight him.'

Domnic stared at Rose, stunned by this simple truth that he hadn't quite grasped for himself. A fight. Of course that was what this was. Hadn't Hal Gryden said as much? He'd said it was time to 'overthrow this police state... dream all the things they won't let us dream about'.

There were butterflies in Domnic's stomach. He felt the way he had the first time he saw Static: as if the future was no longer an unchanging road but an exciting and a terrifying place all at once. There were images crashing into his mind – of freedom, of choices, of adventure. Of anarchy and of blood in the streets. He told himself to resist them. He focused on what was real, what he believed in.

Find Static. Find Hal Gryden. Find the truth.

He hardly noticed when Rose slipped out of the room. 'Bathroom,' she explained.

It was only a ghost image at first, but as Domnic finessed the controls, it came suddenly, sharply into focus. Two figures, young men like himself, sitting on a sofa facing the screen. It was clearly Static: the lack of a channel ident said as much, as did the fact that the actors were wearing black balaclavas so as not to be recognised. Domnic knew the programme; it was one of Gryden's most popular. It belonged to an ancient genre known as the 'situation comedy', but it had been brought bang up to date as a subtle but wicked satire on the influence of the media. It was called *Viewing Figures*.

'*Isn't it funny,*' commented the figure on the left, '*how on TV you only see the police when they're arresting dangerous criminals. You never see them pushing people down the stairs and then shooting them dead because they don't like the look of their face, and then munching on a doughnut, like we all know they do all the time.*'

The remark was greeted by hysterical fake laughter from an unseen audience.

'*I hadn't noticed that,*' said the second figure. '*Guess that's because I'm a brainwashed zombie.*'

'What are you doing?'

The voice was Domnic's first indication that he wasn't alone any more. He hadn't heard the door opening. Still absorbed in the images on the screen, he murmured distractedly, 'I'm watching Static.'

'I can see that. Where are Rose and Jack?'

That one was harder. Domnic had to think about it – and in doing so, he found himself drawn back into the real world, realising only now how long he must have spent submerged in fantasy.

There was a stranger in the room. He leaped to his feet, alarmed.

'Rose and Jack. This is their room. And mine. I'm the Doctor. You must be Domnic.'

'How… how did you…?'

'Because this note was under the door. It's addressed to you. Well? Aren't you going to read it? You can read, can't you?'

'Of course I can… Is this a test or something? Of course I can read. It's allowed. We're allowed magazines and…'

'The note,' said the Doctor slowly, as if addressing an idiot. 'I know that handwriting. Rose could be in danger.'

Domnic took the piece of paper from him and unfolded it. Beneath a letterhead giving the address of the hotel, a few brief words had been scribbled, apparently with an old-fashioned biro: 'Gone with the Doctor to find monsters. Don't wait up. R.'

And underneath, as if it had been an afterthought, 'You see? He *is* real.'

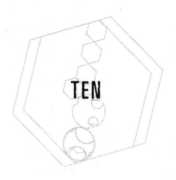

# TEN

The journey to the Big White House passed in heavy silence.

Jack sat wedged between two cops on a wooden bench in the back of a police transport vehicle. The tramp who had called himself Hal Gryden sat opposite, sobbing to himself, avoiding Jack's eye. Jack had been angry with him at first, but as time passed he found himself becoming more sympathetic. When finally he opened his mouth to say something, however – to break the ice – one of the cops jabbed him in the ribs with an elbow and snapped, 'No lying in here!'

The whine of the hoverjets died down and they settled to the ground. An expression of deathly fear came over the tramp's face and he looked as if he might throw up. He had to be carried out like a statue, his whole body frozen.

In contrast, Jack was determined to maintain his dignity. His hands still bound, he needed some help to stand – but as he hopped out of the vehicle, he made an attempt to gain some distance on his escorts, to show that he could walk on his own two feet.

He was surprised to be greeted by a media circus.

The air was thick with steel ball cameras, which whizzed around his head with lenses trained on him, bristling with microphones. Automated lighting units jostled for position, shifting their reflectors to angle bright beams into his face. Almost blinded, Jack could just make out the shapes of reporters and photographers straining against an inadequate cordon of police officers. And then his ears came under assault too, from a babble of raised voices.

'– reporting live from the Big –'

'– Home for the Cognitively –'

'– the police have just brought in the notorious "Armoured Shark Liar" –'

'– charged with twenty-three counts of Fiction in the First –'

'– his lethal charisma –'

'– didn't care who he hurt in the –'

'– ever to see the light of day again –'

He was almost flattered.

There was an athletic-looking woman in his path, chattering to a camera over her shoulder. 'I'm going to try to snatch a few words with this desperate criminal, to find out what motivated Sector Two-Nine-Phi's most appalling storytelling spree on record.' A blonde head whipped around to face Jack. 'Excuse me, sir, do you have anything to say to 8 News? How does it feel to be getting treatment for your disgusting problem?'

'I don't have a problem. Everything I said was the –'

She completely blanked him, turning back to her camera. 'Well, as you could hear there, our sound man was forced to bleep out the detainee's lies. Justice may have caught up with the Armoured Shark Liar, but it seems he is still trying to cause as much mayhem as he can. Ronda Mirthwaite, 8 News, from the Big White House.'

And then Jack was in the hands of the cops again, making no attempt to shrug them off as they guided him firmly through the madness.

Into the asylum.

It was almost a relief to be inside. Certainly, it was quieter in here, though there were more people waiting for him: orderlies in black jumpsuits, standing tensely, flexing their fists, waiting to spring should he prove the smallest threat to their order.

Jack kept very still. He remembered what he had heard about this place, what he'd read for himself on the Ethernet. He knew that its staff had the power to subject him to all manner of unpleasant procedures, should they choose. His best hope was to act the model inmate, give them no excuse.

At least until he could get his bearings and come up with a plan.

The tramp was nowhere to be seen. Evidently, he had been rushed ahead while Jack was getting the full treatment.

A tired-looking white-coated man rushed into the hallway and introduced himself to the cops as Nurse Cal Tyko. He took some cursory details from them – Jack's name, crimes and the name of the arresting officer – and entered them in a data pad without once sparing a glance for Jack himself.

'Mr Jack Harkness,' he repeated to himself as he wrote.

'Captain,' Jack corrected him. 'Captain Jack.'

'Usual place?' asked one of the cops.

Tyko nodded, then caught himself. 'No. No, I'm afraid we don't have a reception cell free at the moment. You've been keeping us busy these past few days.'

'You can't make room? Big catch, this one – you must have seen him on the TV. Liable to turn violent any moment.'

'Actually,' said Jack pointedly, 'I haven't hurt anyone.'

'That's a matter of opinion,' another cop snarled.

'My sister was in one of them pubs where you told your lies. If she goes fantasy crazy…'

'I mean,' said Jack, still addressing Tyko, 'I haven't used violence. I've cooperated fully since my arrest, and I'm sure the officers here will confirm that.'

Tyko raised an eyebrow at the escorting cops and a couple of them nodded reluctantly. Nice to know the no-lying rule could work both ways.

The nurse shone a penlight into Jack's eyes, nodded to himself and made another note on his pad, which he then turned to face Jack. 'What do you see here?'

The pad was displaying an irregular black shape, which looked to Jack like a spaceship orbiting a new world.

'It's a Rorschach inkblot test,' he said.

'And here?'

Tyko waggled a finger and the image changed. This next blot looked like a bronzed hunk reclining on a sun-lounger.

'Ah, yeah,' said Jack with an air of recognition, 'I can see what that is. Another Rorschach inkblot test. It doesn't look like anything. It's a random shape.'

Tyko smiled in approval and took the pad away. 'I think in your case, Mr Harkness, it should be safe to relax the usual formalities. I'll have the orderlies show you to Common Room B until I can spare a moment for your induction interview.'

'Are you sure?' protested one of the cops – the one

with the sister. 'Putting him in with other people? What if he, you know, lies to them?'

'One of the things our patients must learn here, Officer,' said Tyko politely, 'is to resist the many fictions to which they are likely to be exposed.'

'Can I talk to you about God?'

Jack looked up in surprise. No one had said a word to him since he'd been brought into the common room and left with a handful of other inmates, all wearing nightdresses and pyjamas. He'd been sitting alone at a table, thinking. He had hardly noticed the earnest-looking young woman who had taken a seat beside him until now.

'You can talk about anything you like,' he said.

'He is real, you know.'

'I'm sure he is to you, and that's all that matters.'

'He's all that *is* real. The rest of us, the world, this universe, it's all just His great dream – and if we disobey Him, if we turn the dream bad, then He'll wake up and that'll be the end of us all. That's why we mustn't dream for ourselves.' She looked around furtively as if she were committing a terrible deed by voicing the words. Then she brushed her long, straight hair away from her face and added in a stage whisper, 'Because that would mean we're putting ourselves up alongside Him, and that would be blasphemy.'

THE STEALERS OF DREAMS

'Well, it's a point of view,' said Jack.

'All these people around us, they're sinners. They're here because they've dreamed for themselves. Are you a sinner too?'

A dozen answers flooded into Jack's mind, all of them flippant. He suppressed them and said simply, 'I don't think so.' He was being watched, after all. The common room had two doors, and each had a security camera mounted over it and a black-clad orderly standing guard on either side.

One wall was taken up by a TV screen. Of course. About half the inmates present were watching, entranced. One man was sitting cross-legged on the floor, singing under his breath. A woman was giggling and shouting out words at random, about two a minute.

'That's why I'm here,' confided the religious woman. 'It's my mission to save them.'

'I thought you were a –' he wanted to say 'prisoner' – 'patient, like the rest of us. You're wearing a nightdress.'

The woman nodded sadly. 'That's what they think – but everything is God's plan. They say I shouldn't talk about Him because they can't prove He exists, but he *does* exist. He speaks to me. This is where He wants me to be.'

'They've no right,' said Jack angrily. 'You believe what you want to believe.'

'Fish!' shouted the giggling woman.

'God wants me to help them, guide them to the light. They think they're showing me the truth, but it's the other way round.'

'What if –' Jack checked that none of the orderlies were looking in their direction, then continued in a low voice – 'what if we could do more? Wouldn't you like to get out of this place? Resume your work outside?'

The woman shook her head emphatically.

'But if the place is run by, um, sinners… People must talk about it. The other patients, I mean. You must have heard them talking about getting out of here or just changing the way things are run, yeah?'

'Oh, yes – plotting in corners, planning to escape so they can dream and defy God's will again. I always tell the nurses, when I hear them. He won't let them, you see. They can't leave here. This is where they belong. This is where we all belong.' The woman sat back and hugged herself, her eyes filling with melancholy.

'Bum!' shouted the giggler – which summed up Jack's thoughts precisely.

'What makes you think I'm lying?'

Jack leaned back in his chair, affecting an air of nonchalance but fixing his interrogator with a penetrating stare.

Seated across a desk from him in a small office on

the third floor of the Big White House's central block, Tyko sighed wearily. 'You say you weren't born on this world.'

'It's the truth. Can you find any record of me?'

'I suspect that, in fact, you have given us a false name. This in itself suggests a level of disconnection.'

'I'm Captain Jack Harkness. You're Nurse Cal Tyko. This is Colony World 4378976.Delta-Four. You see, I'm perfectly connected.'

'We have your scans, Mr Harkness. We'll find your records.'

'You won't, you know. What is your problem, Cal? Why's this so hard to believe? It's not as if your world has never made First Contact. You came here from Earth. You have documentaries about space travel.'

'Nobody has come to this world since it was founded.'

'I'm not surprised, if this is how you treat your visitors.'

'I find your story improbable in the extreme.'

'And that's the same as "impossible" how?'

'You know the law perfectly well,' said Tyko. 'The onus is on you –'

'To prove it, yeah, yeah. So let me out of here and I will. I'm serious. I can show you my ship. We can even take in the TV cameras if you like.'

'This is getting us nowhere,' said Tyko irritably. 'I need an address from you.'

Jack shrugged. 'Don't have one.'

'And a credit number.'

'Don't have one.'

'You know, it's not too late to give you a shot. I can send for the orderlies.'

'Why? I'm remaining calm. I'm answering your questions.'

'True. But maybe with these fanciful dreams of yours suppressed, you'll feel like answering them truthfully.'

'I'm not dreaming. Wanna know why?'

Tyko sighed and passed a hand over his eyes. 'Tell me why, Mr Harkness.'

'Captain. And the reason I'm not dreaming is that I don't *have* to dream – because I made all *my* dreams come true. You're so keen to know about my childhood – well, guess what I wanted to be when I was a kid? A big-time crook! I wanted the romance, the glamour, the adventure, the thrill of the chase. And you know what? I got all that, but better.'

'Even if I believed you, Mr Harkness –'

'Captain.'

'Even if I believed you, it would not justify your actions. You've no right to spread such stories to the populace. The truth can be as harmful as a lie if it's so far beyond the experience of the listener that it seems like one to him.'

'Yeah, I get that, I do. So take the cameras into my

ship. We'll broadcast the evidence to the world, let them see for themselves. Come on, Cal. You think I've harmed all these people, so let me put things right. Show them the pictures, then they won't have to imagine them, will they?'

'That is quite impossible. I simply don't have the authority –'

'No, I'll just bet you don't – cos that's the last thing you want, isn't it? You, the police, the media… You tell everyone that fiction is dangerous, but the truth is you just don't want them to think about anything – anything they don't have, whether it's real or not.'

'And why do you think that might be, Mr Harkness?' asked Tyko primly.

'To keep them down, in their place. You might not have a government, but I'll just bet there's someone getting very rich and fat somewhere, while the rest of you accept your lot and don't ask for more.'

'You've met some of our other guests. Did they seem rational to you? Did they seem connected? What about the gentleman who was brought in with you? What about him, Mr Harkness?'

'I've told you, it's Captain. And… OK, I don't know. Maybe you're doing something to them. Maybe…'

Tyko had hit on the flaw in Jack's argument, the very point on which his faith had become more and more shaken ever since 'Hal Gryden' had turned out to be a phoney.

'You must realise how paranoid you sound.'

'So I don't have it all worked out yet – but I know one thing. I know there's nothing wrong with having a dream.'

'And that's what you've been doing, isn't it, Mr Harkness? Dreaming. Picturing what's not there, what is not real to you. Maybe you've been reading about the space pioneers and ignoring the warnings, imagining what it would have been like to have flown with them. Or perhaps you've been watching Static. You've been using the right side of your brain, haven't you, Mr Harkness? And you know the right side is the wrong side.'

Somehow, without his words or mannerisms having become any less polite to a fault, Tyko seemed to have become a far more sinister presence.

'What about you?' asked Jack, in a more reasonable tone. 'You must hear stories like mine every day. If fiction's so scary dangerous, how do you cope?'

'Mental discipline, Mr Harkness.'

'I can do that too.'

Tyko glared at him suspiciously.

'Tell me a lie,' said Jack, 'any lie, and I'll show you I can disbelieve it.'

Tyko nodded thoughtfully. 'I suspect that might be the truth.'

Jack leaned forward eagerly. 'Then you accept it can happen? That there are people out there who *can* tell the difference between fact and fiction without your drugs or your "mental discipline"?'

'In rare cases,' Tyko admitted. He reached for a vidphone and punched in three digits. 'And that *being* the case,' he continued, 'I think we can treat you a little differently from our usual guests, Mr Harkness.'

'That's Captain,' said Jack.

They came for him in the corridor.

He'd thought Tyko was taking him back to the common room, but suddenly there were orderlies swarming all over him. Before he knew it, he'd been manhandled onto a trolley and they were strapping him down.

'What's going on?' he protested.

'You've convinced me, Mr Harkness,' said Tyko, as politely as ever. 'You've convinced me that you aren't fantasy crazy.'

'And?'

'And that means your crimes were committed not in a state of confusion but with premeditated malicious intent. You cannot be helped, Mr Harkness – but our laws do allow us to act in the interests of the public, to ensure that you don't offend again.'

'What's that meant to mean?' cried Jack, struggling against his bonds.

'Surgery, Mr Harkness. We are going to burn out the part of your right brain that allows you to visualise, and sever its connection with your language centre on the left. And, as this is a relatively simple procedure and a theatre is available, we are going to carry out the operation immediately. Cheer up, Mr Harkness. Look on the bright side. The average stay of a patient in our facility is three months and two weeks. You'll be free within the hour.'

# ELEVEN

**R**ose fidgeted impatiently as her taxi hovered in a queue of traffic. Over the past hour she'd come to the conclusion that it would have been quicker to walk, but at least the taxi driver knew where she was going.

Or rather, her cab's navigation system did. Every few seconds, it relayed an instruction in a clipped, female tone, occasionally adding a warning, 'Please do not attempt to visualise this route.'

The driver thumped her horn in frustration, swore loudly and revved her hoverjets so that gravel chips flew up from the road to spatter the windows.

None of these aggravations mattered, though, because the Doctor was back.

Just the sight of him, sitting alongside her, made Rose smile. She still had that flaming itch in the back of her brain, somewhere to the right, but she wasn't confused any more. The Doctor made everything seem clear.

She'd felt a bit guilty about abandoning Domnic, but the Doctor had insisted. 'He's another Mickey,' he had said, 'or an Adam. Like most of the apes that evolved from your planet. He wouldn't cope.' Rose had been torn, as she always was when he said things like that, between feeling slighted at the insult to her species and flattered because he had made her an exception.

He had soon cheered her up. She had laughed at his efforts to flag down a cab, jumping, waving, even haring out into the roadway and hammering on the windscreen of one that was stuck at a junction. It was as if the drivers couldn't see him. As if he was invisible. She had stuck two fingers in her mouth and whistled and a black vehicle had pulled up straight away.

'Where's it to be?' the driver had asked from the other side of her glass partition as they'd climbed into the back.

'Where are we going, Doctor?' Rose had mumbled.

'Big White House,' he'd said.

'Eh? Didn't catch that. Speak up, luv.'

'The Big White House,' Rose had repeated loudly.

'So what's the plan?' she asked the Doctor now.

'Depends what we find when we get there.'

'But the usual, yeah? Beat the monsters, put things right, set everyone free.'

He grinned. 'Oh yeah.' And he took her by the hand, and she felt electricity flowing through her body, and she was grinning too.

'So why the Big White House?' she asked.

'No government,' he said, 'so who d'you think is keeping the people down, enforcing the status quo?'

'The police?'

'Guess again.'

Rose thought for a moment. 'The media. The newspapers and the TV.'

'Bingo!'

'Like on Satellite Five.'

'If you like.'

'Is that what's happening? Is it the Jagrafess again?'

'Doubt it. Wrong time period. Anyway, when we last saw the Mighty Jagrafess of the Hadro-um-something Maxa-whatchamacallit, he was cooked meat. Doesn't mean he was the first alien monster to cotton on to the power of the human media.'

'As a brainwashing tool, right?'

'As a means of spreading ideas, reinforcing a selective viewpoint. The question is, whose ideas? Whose viewpoint? If the media controls the people, who controls the media?'

'Bet Hal Gryden knows.'

'I'll bet he does. He's playing the official channels at their own game. S'pose he knows what he's doing. I prefer the direct approach myself.'

'The TV studios,' realised Rose. She thought for a moment, then looked at the Doctor. 'Only, that's not where we're going…'

It took him a moment to answer. Maybe he was just giving her time to work it out for herself. 'There are too many studios, too many publishing companies, too many people between us and the real power. This way's faster. If you want to find a tyrant, follow the dissidents.'

'To the Big White House.'

'That's where they take the people who still dare to dream. That's where some of them learn to toe the line, and the others… Well, let's see.'

'Big White House,' said the taxi driver in a surly tone, bringing them to a halt on a surprisingly quiet road. 'And I hope you've come to check yourself in, luv. All that talk of satellites and jagra fish…'

'Oi,' said Rose, 'that was a private conversation. You weren't meant to be listening.'

'Couldn't help hearing your side of it, luv. That'll be two credits thirty.'

The Doctor dug out his card wallet. 'I think this explains everything,' he said, flashing it in the driver's direction. She said nothing, just continued to glower at Rose. The Doctor looked chagrined. 'Psychic paper's not working, Rose.'

'Well, try something else,' she whispered, squirming under the driver's glare.

'Two credits thirty,' she repeated sternly.

'Haven't you got any money?'

'Hadn't really thought,' said the Doctor.

'Oh, that's enough!' snapped the driver, starting the engine again. 'I knew I shoulda left you standing – one look and I could tell you were fantasy crazy. Well, you're coming back to the depot with me, luv. We'll sort this out there, give you a proper taste of reality.'

'Doctor! What do we do?'

'When all else fails, Rose… leg it!'

They reached for the doors – but at that moment Rose heard the solid thunks of safety locks engaging, and the taxi's engines screamed as it sped away from the kerb with an acceleration that pushed her back into her seat. Simultaneously, a steel shield slid down in front of the driver's partition.

'Sonic screwdriver!' cried Rose.

'Out of juice,' said the Doctor. 'I've been meaning to recharge the power pack.'

'Fat lot of use you're being today!'

He was hammering on the window in his door with both fists, to no avail.

'Here, brace me!' said Rose, twisting around in her seat until she could attack the window next to her with her feet. The driver let out a cry of protest as her third double-heeled kick did the trick. She manoeuvred herself back into a sitting position and knocked shards of glass out of the frame with her elbow.

The taxi took a corner wide and came up against another traffic jam. While it was stalled, Rose reached through the broken window and fumbled for the handle outside. To her relief, the door gave, and she and the Doctor spilled out onto the pavement.

'You won't get away with this, you crazy geek!' the taxi driver was screaming. 'I've got your DNA on my seat, I'll find you!'

They raced back in the direction of the Big White House, a stream of curses ringing in their ears.

'You sure you can do this?' asked the Doctor dubiously.

'Champion gymnast, remember. Just give me a bunk-up.'

They were standing at the back of the Big White House, beside the three-metre-high wall that ringed the property. Normally, they'd have bluffed their way in through the front gate, but after the taxi Rose had suggested a sneakier approach.

The Doctor laced his fingers into a basket, then she stepped on it and let him propel her upwards. She reached for the top of the wall and thought she had it, but the next thing she knew she was back on the pavement, stumbling and almost falling.

'What the hell just happened?' she complained.

'Don't look at me,' said the Doctor. 'Ever thought of cutting down on the chips?'

'Oi, less of the cheek, you!'

They tried a second and a third time – but again the Doctor's hands just seemed to part beneath her foot to leave her back where she'd started.

'Oh, honestly, Doctor,' groaned Rose. 'I bet you throw like a girl too.'

They found a bin in an alleyway across the road, waited till no one was looking and pinched it. They wheeled it up to the wall and Rose climbed onto it. The Doctor was meant to be holding the bin steady, but it almost slipped out from under her.

Now, though, she could reach the top of the wall with a short jump. Her hands clamped onto it…

… and a jolt of something cold stabbed up through her arms, into her chest and stomach. Rose gasped, lost her grip, fell, landed hard on the bin and bounced onto the pavement.

'Ah,' said the Doctor.

'Ah, what?' she snapped at him, verging on mutiny. She picked herself up, waving aside his offer of a helping hand.

'Ah, I thought there might be something like that. Force field, from the look of it. A more advanced alternative to barbed wire. You OK?'

'I'm OK – and thanks for the warning.'

'Looks like it's back to Plan A,' said the Doctor brightly.

'The front gate,' said Rose. 'OK, how about you

pretend to be a doctor and I'm a nurse?'

'Wouldn't work. They'll have ways of checking, and without the psychic paper...'

'Yeah, what was up with that anyway?'

The Doctor shrugged. 'Maybe there's something about these people, makes them immune.'

'Something our monster did to them.'

'Could explain why so many of them go "fantasy crazy".'

There was a short, awkward silence. Rose wondered if this was the time to come clean, to tell him about her own delusional episode. But she felt much better now and the zombies seemed like a long-faded dream.

'S'pose we could say we're visiting someone,' she suggested. 'A patient.'

'I don't know,' said the Doctor. 'If half of what we suspect about this place is true, I doubt they put out the red carpet for visitors.'

'Well, d'you have any ideas?'

'Yeah. I can think of one sure way of getting into a lunatic asylum.'

It took Rose a moment to latch on to his train of thought, then she grinned. 'Oh, you're joking!'

'So, which of us do you think'll make the best lunatic?'

'It came on all of a sudden like,' explained Rose to the

bored guard at the gate. 'He thinks he's a doctor.'

'I think I'm *the* Doctor.' The Doctor fixed the guard with his most manic grin.

'He thinks he… he's 900 years old and he flies around the universe fighting farting aliens and pigs in space.'

'I want locking up, I do,' said the Doctor. 'I'm mad as a March hare, daft as a brush.'

'You should take him to see your community physician,' said the guard.

'Oh… yeah, yeah, I know that, but he's away, you see. Some conference on the other side of town. Anyway, he's got a backlog. We can't get an appointment for two weeks.'

'Padded cell. Straitjacket. Throw away the key for all I care.'

Rose leaned closer to the guard, conspiratorially. 'Thing is, he's got this barmy idea that there's a monster in this building.' She had hoped to get a reaction to that, but the guard's expression didn't flicker at all. 'It was either bring him here or wait for the police to do it. I mean, you've gotta see he needs help, urgent like.'

The Doctor walked up to the guard and stood so close that their noses almost touched through the bars of the gate. He stared at him intently for a moment, then broke out into an animated impression of a chimpanzee.

The guard looked right through him, his attention fixed on Rose. 'Yes, ma'am,' he said tiredly, 'I reckon I do see that some form of medical intervention is needed here. Maybe you should go through to the house after all.'

Rose could hardly keep a big grin off her face as the guard opened the gate and waved her through. She couldn't look at the Doctor at all, for fear that she would burst out laughing. They walked side by side down a path towards the Big White House itself, but they were still only halfway there when he muttered in her ear, 'You realise he'll have called ahead, don't you?'

'They'll be waiting for us.'

'On the plus side,' said the Doctor cheerfully, 'getting captured usually works – gives us a short cut to the big bad guy. Or we could…'

Rose glanced back over her shoulder. The guard had returned to a little booth just inside the gate. She could see him through a window, with his back to her, apparently talking to someone on a vidphone. She looked at the Doctor and they smiled at each other. He offered his hand and she took it.

They broke away from the path at a joyous run.

They found a door leading into the left-hand wing of the Big White House, but it was locked and didn't seem to have been opened in months. Round the back of the building, two people in white kitchen overalls chatted outside another door, and Rose and the Doctor pulled back before they could be seen.

Beside them a row of windows gave access to a wood-panelled passageway. Rose tried one, but this too was locked. So were the second and the third – and as soon as she touched the fourth, an alarm began to shriek. She thought she'd set it off at first, but the Doctor pointed out that the staff inside had probably just noticed the disappearance of their new patient and his escort.

'They know we're in the grounds, but they don't know where yet. Should give us a minute or so.'

'You could help, y'know,' said Rose as she tugged at a fourth window in vain. She could have screamed with frustration. She hadn't realised how much she had come to rely on the Doctor's bag of tricks to take them anywhere, any time he pleased.

He wandered up to a window that she'd already tried and peered through it. Without looking, he pointed to the left and said, 'Next along but one. Looks like a broken latch.' He was right.

Rose was clambering onto the window sill when the first orderlies came racing around the corner. One of them shouted something, but she couldn't hear it over the incessant alarm. She scrambled into the building and turned to help the Doctor, but it was too late. He ran, just inches ahead of the orderlies' reaching hands. A couple of them began to climb in after Rose, while two more set off after the Doctor towards the kitchen door.

Rose soon lost sight of them as she made two turns at random, hoping to shake off her pursuers, looking for a place to hide. Her heart sank as she spotted a spherical camera in a ceiling corner, rotating to follow her.

The Doctor was suddenly beside her. Rose couldn't imagine how he'd got here so quickly – he must have found another way in. She saw no sign of the orderlies who'd been following him, but they couldn't be far behind. She could hear more footsteps and raised voices from the right, so the Doctor took her hand again and led her to the left. Normally she would have felt safer by his side, whatever the situation, but this time there was something nagging at her. Something wrong.

A large, arched wooden door was standing ajar and the Doctor made for it. They crashed into what appeared to be a patients' common room. People were sitting around, hollow-eyed, slow to react to their appearance. The same, unfortunately, could not be said of the orderlies inside the door – or of those who stood guard at another door, opposite.

Rose was herded into the centre of the room, a ring of black uniforms closing in. She had nowhere else to go, so she leaped up onto a table, causing a man who'd been leaning on it with his head in his arms to fall off his chair in surprise.

Simultaneously, another man threw himself at an orderly, with a desperate plea, 'Help me! I can see them again! I can see the pretty girls again!'

A young woman with long, straight hair slapped him across the face. 'Sinner!' she spat. 'Parading your smutty dreams in here for all to see!'

'Formica!' shouted another woman, before collapsing into a giggling fit.

It was taking one orderly to subdue the distressed man, another to keep the straight-haired woman away from him. Rose made for the gap between them and broke through, the far door in sight. She barrelled through into another long, straight corridor...

... but there were more orderlies ahead of her, coming for her.

She threw herself at the nearest door, feeling a surge of hope as it opened, finding that hope dashed at the sight of a cleaning cupboard, empty but for an overturned bottle of bleach on the top shelf.

And then she was overrun, and the orderlies' hands were grasping at her, pulling her down, and she was trying to fight, but for every hand she batted away there were two to replace it, and that alarm was shrieking like a drill in her head, and the itch in her brain had flared up into a ball of pain.

As she was forced onto her knees, Rose caught one last glimpse of her trusted companion standing above her, seemingly unconcerned.

'Doctor, do something!' she spluttered.

'Can't.' He shrugged. 'I thought you knew – I'm invisible.'

And then she was lying face down on a white floor on which the recent application of a mop had just made wet dirt patterns, and the weight of three, four, five bodies was holding her down, and the alarm stopped at last and the world seemed to fall into a deathly hush as, out of the corner of her eye, Rose caught sight of the gleam of a sharp needlepoint…

… and felt it pricking into the side of her neck.

# TWELVE

'**D**'you wanna come with me?' Domnic couldn't describe how he had felt when he heard those words. It was as if, in the few seconds he'd been in his life, the Doctor had changed it for ever. As if the future he'd been waiting for had arrived at last.

It had taken Domnic those few seconds to adjust to the fact that this man, this stranger – this… this normal-looking bloke – was the one about whom Rose had said so much. Despite her protestations, he had still half thought of her Doctor as a fiction. Now, transfixed by a pair of intense blue eyes, he remembered spaceships and time travel and monsters and…

He knew he shouldn't have believed, but… but…

*'D'you wanna come with me?'*

He had timed it to perfection. He had read Rose's note – the one that Domnic still didn't understand;

the one that said she had gone off with him – and he had scowled and muttered, 'Not her.' His shoulders stooped as if carrying a great weight, he had turned and left the hotel room. He might have forgotten that Domnic was there.

Just enough time had passed. Enough for Domnic to realise that, wherever this stranger was going, he had to be there. Enough to fear that, if he let the Doctor walk out now, he would be throwing away everything he'd ever wanted. So what if it was a lie? He couldn't sleep until he knew for sure.

Just enough time for him to realise that he didn't have the words.

And then the Doctor had paused, one hand still on the half-open door, and he had looked at Domnic as if noticing him for the first time. His expression had cleared and he had issued his invitation – at exactly the right moment, before the doubts and the fears had begun to set in.

The only moment at which the invitation could have been accepted.

So now Domnic was outside the city for the first time, wading through a lush jungle that he had only glimpsed in natural history programmes and his dreams, and it was as if he had found a whole new world already.

There were colours he had never seen in the city and shapes that seemed at once gloriously random and yet meticulously plotted. But there were roots pulling at his feet too, thorns snagging on his jumpsuit and branches scratching his hands and face. And the always-present sense of danger, the fear that some predator could leap from the foliage at any moment.

Not that there *were* any predators. There were no indigenous life forms at all on Colony World 4378976.Delta-Four. That was why it had been so perfect for settlement. But Domnic's comic strips had often used the jungle as a backdrop and filled it with beasts from his darkest dreams. The jungle represented the unknown, the unexplored – and no matter how many scans had confirmed it empty, there was always the tiny, tiny possibility that the scans were wrong. That something was hiding.

He tried not to think about it. If he did, he would hear them. He would hear the crunching of footsteps behind him, the rasping of breath as something waited in ambush. He would catch signs of movement in the corner of his eye – a creeper disturbed here, a leaf shaken from a branch there – and he would know that the monsters were waiting.

He focused on the Doctor instead. As they'd set out on their journey, Rose's friend had fired off a barrage of questions, about Domnic, about his life and his dealings with Rose and Captain Jack. That had helped him. Talking about things he remembered, real things, had anchored him, kept him from being overwhelmed by the possibilities of the new. Once the Doctor had his answers, though, he had lapsed into a silence that had at first been contemplative but now just seemed sullen.

Domnic needed that anchor again, so he ventured, 'It's like something out of a storybook, isn't it?'

'No,' said the Doctor shortly.

'Oh, I... I mean, I'm not saying they're real, the stories, I just... What if they... Well, what if they were? Because how can we be sure? Really sure?'

'They're not real.'

'I can show you, if you like. One of my comic strips.'

The Doctor froze and looked at Domnic for a moment. He seemed to consider his offer, but then a smile tugged at his lips and he said, 'No ta. Not interested.' And he ploughed on.

A minute later, the Doctor asked, 'Why do you keep doing that?'

'What?'

'Pinching yourself. You just did it again.'

'Oh. I hadn't realised. A reflex, that's all.'

'Helps you concentrate?'

'I guess, yeah. It's just... all this, I'm finding it a bit hard to, you know... The jungle. You. If I pinch myself, I can feel the pain and I know I'm not dreaming. You must have heard... I mean, it's what people do, right?'

'It's what they say,' said the Doctor, 'but no one actually does it. No need. If you're dreaming, yeah, sometimes the mind can be fooled, the dream can seem real, but it doesn't work the other way round. When something's real, you just know. Otherwise you'd be knocked flat by the first bus to appear round a blind corner while you're still stood in the middle of the road telling yourself how improbable it all is.'

'How?' asked Domnic. '*How* do you tell the difference? Because I've had dreams like this before, and they've looked like this and sounded like this and smelt and felt like this and I've *wanted* them to be real, but I've still woken up and… Sometimes, I think *that* might be the dream, my bedroom, and I'm pinching myself and I'm trying to go back to the jungle or the spaceship or the zombie castle or… or…'

'What an exciting life you must lead.'

'Not really,' said Domnic with a sigh, 'because it never changes. Whatever I dream, whatever I write down, it's always a lie.'

'That's what happens,' said the Doctor, 'when you just wait for change instead of making it happen. What you're about to see, by the way – it's real.'

There was something in front of them. A new shade among the jungle colours; hard, straight lines that belonged to the city, the domain of humans.

A chunky, fat cabinet, nestled between the trees. A rich, dark blue. Some sort of a store shed? But why all the way out here? And why did it display, in bright, backlit letters, the legend 'POLICE PUBLIC CALL BOX'?

Domnic's mind raced, trying to find the logic in the blue box's presence – because, without that logic, he was afraid he would wake up again.

'Go to it,' said the Doctor, beaming like a proud uncle. 'Touch it.'

Domnic ran his hands over the cabinet's surface, concentrating on the feel of the wood on his skin. It was rough, solid, real. And there was more.

Something behind the wood. Something that Domnic couldn't quite feel with his fingers, couldn't describe, but it was there. Something powerful, straining to get out. It was intangible, unknowable, and yet he was sure that it was real too.

'And while you're there,' said the Doctor, 'have a good walk round, get used to the size of it. It'll save you some time later on.'

It was a dream after all.

There was no other explanation, no way that the doors of the blue cabinet could really have opened into the room that Domnic was now seeing.

His first impression was that the huge, round chamber was alive – as alive as the jungle outside. Coral clung to its walls, support beams twisted and branched like trees, cables hung like creepers and trailed like roots along the floor. But there were ceramic handrails and metal grille flooring beneath Domnic's feet, and a mushroom-shaped control bank that looked as if it had been gutted and rebuilt out of spare parts.

Had it not been for his disappointment that none of this was real, he could have been proud of himself. It looked as if his mind had spewed up images from throughout his life, from everything he had ever seen on the TV, and crammed them together at random and yet somehow, impossibly, made the whole thing work.

When he woke up, he was going to write a great story about this.

For now, he let the Doctor – a mass of energy and authority who still seemed obdurately, impossibly real – lead him past the console, past an incongruous chair and through a doorway. Expecting to emerge from the back of the cabinet, Domnic laughed to himself and shook his head to find three corridors stretching away from him, more corridors criss-crossing them. The walls had the same organic, encrusted look as the ones behind him.

They took one turning after another, their route twisting and looping back on itself until Domnic had lost all sense of direction. The Doctor was thoughtful, as if he couldn't quite remember where he had left something. Then he braked sharply outside a door, pushed it open and announced, 'This'll do!'

This room was round too, but mercifully small, cluttered with an assortment of junk as eclectic as the lash-ups in the main chamber. Much of it appeared to be medical in nature and most had been patched up in some way or another. An ECG monitor had been left to rot on a trolley, wires hanging out of its back, while a bench was festooned with bottles and syringes, and a stethoscope lay draped over a battered refrigeration unit.

The Doctor swept a box-shaped machine from a dentist's chair, not seeming to care that it hit the floor with a crash and a tinkle of broken glass. He gestured to his guest to take a seat, but Domnic balked at the prospect.

'Hang on – what are you planning to do to me?'

The Doctor shrugged. 'Quick examination. Nothing to get your knickers in a knot about. I just want to see why your brain doesn't work the same as other humans'.' He grinned disarmingly and bounced on his toes – but his hands were behind his back and Domnic didn't know what he had just picked up.

'You're a doctor, aren't you!'

'*The* Doctor. Not the same thing.'

'And this… this… whatever it is… this police box. Police box! I should have seen… I was right last night, when I first… You're working with them, aren't you!'

'Er… no.'

'You want to open up my head and… and zap out bits of my brain.'

'There's no need to exaggerate.'

'You even *sound* like the police! I… I don't care if this *is* a dream, I won't let you…'

Domnic backed away, but in his panic he found the wall instead of the door. And the Doctor was upon him, taking him by the shoulder, guiding him firmly into the chair – and before Domnic could recover his wits, could do anything more than just dig his fingernails into his palms and hope to *wake up*, the Doctor had kicked a lever at the base of the chair so that it collapsed into a horizontal position. And then he was holding a bulky brass contraption, like a diver's helmet studded with control knobs, and Domnic was still flailing, trying to straighten himself as the helmet came down over his head and he felt its weight on his shoulders, the chill of its metal against the exposed parts of his neck.

'Best think of something nice,' cautioned the Doctor. 'This might hurt a bit.'

The jungle looked different, though Domnic didn't know why.

He *felt* different – light-headed, as if some great pressure had been taken off his mind.

The Doctor had busied himself about the helmet contraption, adjusting controls, clicking his tongue and occasionally asking Domnic if he could feel anything. Most of the time, there had just been a low-level buzz in his head – though there had been one worrying moment when a circuit or something had blown out and the Doctor had attacked the helmet enthusiastically with a strange sort of soldering iron that gave off blue light.

Then, with no warning at all, something had sparked and sent an electrical pain through Domnic's head, causing him to cry out. The current had seemed to shudder through his entire skeleton, making his body tighten.

'Still think you're dreaming?' the Doctor asked now. He had been walking six steps ahead of Domnic, but he'd suddenly turned to face him.

'No… Yeah… I don't know.'

'Imagine something for me.'

'What? Like what?'

'Something in the jungle. A monster.'

'I don't want to.'

'Aw, come on, Derek.'

'Domnic.'

'You're supposed to be a writer, aren't you? Give me a story. Vast jungle like this, there's bound to be something in here, don't you think?' The Doctor was right in Domnic's face, smiling, but there was a malicious gleam in his eyes. 'Cos I'm sure I heard something a few metres back, you know. Sort of footsteps, padding after us. Could be zombies.'

Domnic swallowed nervously. 'I didn't hear anything.'

'Yeah, you did, you just don't want to admit it in case I think you're fantasy crazy. But that's not very bright, is it, Daniel? Not bright at all, because what if the monsters are real? And they could be, you know.'

'Stop it!' cried Domnic.

'Creeping up on us right now, and what good are you gonna be when they pounce? Standing there with your fingers in your ears and your eyes closed.'

'No! I... I... You're right, I can hear them! I can see them! I...'

The zombies, crashing out of the bushes, their arms outstretched.

'... can see... them...'

And yet, at the same time, they *weren't* there.

'... in my mind. I can see them in my mind, but...'

But, to Domnic's astonishment, that was all.

'Result!' crowed the Doctor.

'What... what... what do you...'

'You're cured! For the time being, anyway.'

'Cured? Cured of what?'

'Micro-organisms,' announced the Doctor, 'smaller than a single proton, thriving in the atmosphere of this world. They're all around us. They were in your brain – until the feedback from my scanner drove them out. Won't work for ever, though. Give it a few hours, they'll be back.'

'You… you mean…' Domnic put a hand to his head, tried to concentrate. They were still in there, the zombies, but trapped somewhere deep down, where they couldn't get out.

He felt a sudden rush of fear. 'You've taken them from me. How can I… I can't feel my dreams any more, how can I write again? What have you done to me?'

The Doctor looked put out by his ingratitude. 'You'll get used to it,' he sniffed. 'Your dreams might be less vivid now, but they're safe. You can dream bigger dreams, without being afraid. Who knows? You might even dream something worthwhile, one day.'

And then he was off again, crashing through the jungle so that Domnic had to scramble to keep up with him even as his mind was racing to make sense of what he had said. Micro-organisms? What did that mean? It sounded like fiction to him – it sounded like *science* fiction – but there was no doubt that the Doctor had done something to him, *changed* something.

And he found himself wondering what it would be like to be able to dream like the Doctor. To *be* like him. Or like Rose Tyler – to travel with this strange and wonderful man in his blue cabinet. To have his mind blown like this every day. To be the Doctor's friend, his assistant, his companion.

Somehow, he just couldn't imagine it.

# THIRTEEN

He had left it too late to struggle. By the time he realised what they were doing to him, he had been too badly outnumbered. His chances of getting away had been practically zero. So he'd kept up the pretence of cooperating with them, for a second too long.

Until Nurse Tyko had told him what would happen next.

And then Jack had struggled all right, pulling with all his strength at the straps that secured his wrists above his head to the cold metal trolley. It had taken the orderlies minutes to catch his kicking feet and to strap down his ankles, and he had given them a few good bruises in the process.

He hadn't cried out, though, hadn't shouted in anger or begged for mercy. He hadn't wasted his strength.

Tyko escorted him as far as the lift. As the doors rumbled shut between them, Jack strained his stomach muscles to lift his head, to shoot one final look of contempt at the young nurse. He wasn't sure what reaction to expect. Would he be ashamed and look away? Or would he gloat over his victory?

He did neither. Tyko's eyes were blank, neither happy nor sad about Jack's fate. As if it meant nothing to him: another day, another name on his pad.

The lift doors opened again and Jack was wheeled out into the less sterile surroundings of the ground floor – the old part of the house, where the squeak of the trolley's front left wheel was softened by carpet. The ceiling was wood-timbered and the lights left blurred trails in front of his eyes as they rolled by.

Then strips of a heavy, transparent plastic batted briefly about his head and he was in a different part of the asylum altogether. A new part, one of the extensions he had seen from outside. A part where the walls and the ceiling, like those in the central block, were a dirty off-white, where an antiseptic smell filled the air along with a faint whiff of ozone.

And a part where somebody was screaming, yelling their throat raw. Then the scream gave way to a plaintive whimper, which subsided in turn.

Jack could almost have believed that the sounds had been staged – a way of heightening his anticipation of what was to come – except that anticipation was probably illegal here.

This wasn't happening. No way did Captain Jack Harkness go out like this. He was fated to die in a blaze of glory, at a time and place of his own choosing – when and where it really mattered – not to live out his days as a vegetable on some backwater world. He was sure of that, confident in his own abilities. He would get out of this. He just didn't know how yet.

He hadn't struggled when they bound his wrists. But he had, instinctively, tensed his muscles and held his clenched fists as far away from the trolley as he could. The orderlies had thought they'd yanked his straps tight, but Jack had gained a little leeway around his right wrist. Just a little, no more. He'd been pulling on the strap ever since, surreptitiously. He had been able to work it up to the base of his thumb, but it wouldn't slide over.

He was wheeled into a basic operating theatre, where a red sterilising light cast everything in a harsh glare. Against it, the face of his surgeon was a hazy shadow with his nose and mouth obscured by a half-mask – but Jack had no problems seeing the tool he was wielding.

The surgeon thumbed a switch on the side of the pen-sized device and a thin wire extruded from it, its end flaring alight like a captured miniature star.

'I don't want you to worry,' said the surgeon. 'I'm just going to thread this wire up your nose. The brain has no pain receptors, so you shouldn't feel a thing. It's a simple procedure, not very delicate at all. It'll be over in seconds and you'll retain control over most of your bodily functions.'

'You oughtta know,' bluffed Jack, 'I'm a time agent, come here to investigate why this planet of yours is so backward. Harm me and you'll have a hundred warships up your butt before you can blink.'

'Yes, well, Mr Harkness,' said the surgeon, not unkindly, 'that's exactly the sort of lie we'll be hoping not to hear from you again.'

And he leaned forward, until the glowing end of the wire filled Jack's world.

Jack was pulling on the loose strap with all his might, in danger of wrenching his right thumb from its socket, not caring if he did. But even if he could get one hand free, what good would it do him? He'd hoped the orderlies would have left by now, but they were standing around, on guard. Six of them plus the surgeon.

Fortunately, Jack wasn't alone either.

He knew, as soon as he heard the shriek of the alarm, that the Doctor or Rose, and maybe both, would be behind it. He was still getting used to that: to the fact that he didn't have to pull the rabbit out of his own hat every time now.

The orderlies checked their pagers and looked at each other, uncertain whether to answer the call if it meant leaving their infamous prisoner unguarded. The surgeon, his burning light no longer in Jack's eyes, made the choice for them, chivvying them out. 'If this patient ever was a danger to me,' he insisted, 'he won't be for much longer.'

With a squelching of bones, Jack finally pulled his hand free. He wrapped the empty strap around his fingers, trying to disguise what he'd done. Until the surgeon leaned over him again.

Then Jack tried to snatch his pen device – but the surgeon reacted just too fast, pulling away, backing out of the range of Jack's next swipe, calling for help.

Jack just hoped the alarm was too loud for the surgeon's voice to be heard, hoped that he could free his other limbs before the orderlies came back.

He was still fumbling with the strap around his other wrist when the surgeon lunged at him, brandishing a liquid-filled hypodermic. Some sort of anaesthetic, no doubt. Jack caught his attacker's arm before the needle could puncture his skin, but he was struggling one-handed against two – and the force of his efforts was so great that his trolley tipped onto its side, crashing to the floor with a jarring impact, so that Jack was splayed vertically like a mounted fish.

The surgeon had lost his grip on the hypo. It skittered to the floor beside Jack, who crushed it with his fist. While the surgeon was rushing to prepare another dose, Jack untied his left hand and made short work of his ankle straps.

The surgeon was coming at him again, and Jack grabbed the trolley and raised it above his head as a shield. Scrambling to his feet, he drove his attacker backwards into the clear door of a freezer cabinet, rattling the bottles within. While the surgeon was winded, Jack dropped the trolley and floored him with a punch to the jaw.

He whirled around to greet two returning orderlies.

The fight was short but sweet, and Jack won it by two knockouts. But the alarm siren had cut off and he knew his distraction was over.

He righted the trolley on which he'd been bound, then threw a sheet over the top so that it hung to the floor and concealed the unconscious orderlies beneath. The surgeon he hid behind the freezer cabinet. He picked their key cards from their hip pouches and considered taking an orderly's uniform – but they were both shorter and narrower around the shoulders than he was.

Jack found a roll of surgical tape and wrapped up his three prisoners, tying their hands behind their backs and covering their mouths.

He locked the doors of the operating theatre behind him, checking through their small round windows that no one could be seen, that the room looked empty. Then he hurried to where he thought the scream had come from. He found another theatre but this one was closed too. He shivered at the thought that it had claimed its victim and appreciated the timing of the alarm that had saved him more than ever.

He knew where he was going. Even strapped to the trolley, he had memorised his route on the way in, mindful of the likely need for a quick escape. He soon found his way back to the hanging plastic blinds through which he'd been pushed and into the main part of the house. He took cover as two orderlies walked by, talking animatedly about the state of the world today, about how more and more people were being lured into fiction use.

He was creeping down a carpeted corridor, the front door only two turns away, when he saw Rose.

Two orderlies had her arms. Two more were standing behind her. As Jack watched, they carried her into a lift. Rose was awake, but not fighting. Her expression was vacant. She was dragging her left leg as she tried to walk – and a terrible fear knotted Jack's stomach.

What if they had done to her what they'd tried to do to him? What if it had been her scream he had heard?

No, he reassured himself. It had been a man's voice, he was sure. And chances were it had been Rose who had sparked the alarm, in which case they hadn't had time… They had probably just given her a 'shot', as Tyko had put it.

The lift doors closed and Jack hurried over to check the floor indicator, to see where they were taking her. It stopped on the fourth floor of the central block.

He looked around for the stairs.

Jack waited for the orderlies to move away from the door. They turned and came back to the lift, at last, and he darted back into the stairwell until they had passed.

Then he sprinted for the dorm into which they had taken Rose.

He ran the surgeon's key card through the reader – the wrong way round, as it happened. A light flickered red. And there were footsteps, coming towards him. Someone was about to round the corner – and, stuck in the middle of the corridor like this, Jack had nowhere to hide.

He fumbled with the card again, cursing under his breath and wishing he'd tried to squeeze himself into an orderly's jumpsuit after all.

The lock disengaged and he almost fell through the door. As he closed it behind him, Rose looked up from the room's single bed where she lay, hugging herself. Her eyes were red and swollen, but hope ignited in them as she saw him.

Then it was gone, replaced by confusion and suspicion.

'Jack? Is that really you? Tell me it's you.' The words were laboured and a little slurred, as if it was an effort to say them.

He put a finger to his lips, silencing her, as the footsteps approached down the corridor. He crouched with his back flat against the door, so he couldn't be seen when the barred hatch above him opened.

He would have recognised Cal Tyko's voice even if the nurse hadn't introduced himself. 'And your name is?'

Rose didn't say anything. She raised herself onto her elbows, favouring her right side, blinking in the light of the room's enormous TV screen. She looked at Tyko – and then, to Jack's horror, she looked directly at him.

'Who were you talking to?'

Rose returned her gaze to the nurse.

'Just now. Don't lie to me, I heard you as I came along the corridor. You were talking to someone.'

A short silence, during which Jack held his breath.

'You know there's nobody in here, don't you?' said Tyko. He had only to try the door, to find it unlocked, and the game would be up. Jack could take him out, of course, but not before he raised the alarm – and there were orderlies all over this part of the asylum.

Rose looked at Jack again, then she seemed to make a decision that came as a relief to her. 'Yeah. Yeah, I know that.' She sank back into her mattress.

In a more kindly tone, Tyko said, 'I know this must be disconcerting for you. The medicine doesn't last long and it's wearing off. You're starting to imagine things again. If it gets too much, we can give you another shot, but it's far better if you can overcome these delusions by yourself.'

'No one else here,' muttered Rose sleepily.

'There'll be a reception cell free in an hour or so,' said Tyko. 'I'll send the orderlies to collect you and we can have a little chat, yes? Then I'll be able to help you.'

The hatch closed and Tyko's footsteps echoed away.

Jack breathed out, whistling through his teeth. 'Close thing.'

'Go away,' said Rose, turning her back to him.

'Rose?'

'I said go away. You're not real!'

'Hey, hey!' He crossed the room and laid a hand on her shoulder. She flinched. 'It's me. Captain Jack. "Not real"? You tell that to the guys I had to lay out to get this far.'

She was studiously ignoring him.

'Tell you what, if I can get you of here, will you believe I'm the genuine article?' He showed Rose his stolen key cards and the hope returned to her eyes. Jack fanned out the three cards with a grin. 'I'm building up a collection.'

'I need you to tell me something. You've heard of the Jagrafess, yeah?'

'The Mighty Jagrafess?'

'Yeah.'

'Of the Holy Hadrojassic Maxarodenfoe?'

Rose was grinning now too. 'That'd be the one. You *are* real! Oh, God, you're real!' They hugged each other, but suddenly Rose pulled away and her smile faded. 'The Doctor… I was with him…'

'Was he captured too? Is he around here somewhere?'

Rose shook her head. 'You don't understand. He wasn't really here at all. When they put that needle in me, he just… faded… like a ghost… Jack, what's up?'

He had straightened and was pacing with his fist to his lips, his brow furrowed. 'You're right, I don't. I don't understand.' He turned back to Rose. 'If it can happen to us too… They call it "fantasy crazy". That's what you're telling me, right? You've been seeing things that aren't there.'

'I s'pose, yeah.'

'Like the doctors and the police have been saying all along. Did they do something to you, Rose? Is that it?'

'I don't *think*…'

'When did it start? When did you first see this ersatz Doctor? Was it after you came to the Big White House?'

Rose screwed up her face in concentration. 'We got

separated. I was running along and he was just there. I didn't know how he'd… I mean, he could have been real before then, I s'pose, but… No. No, I don't think he was. In the taxi… The way nothing he did seemed to work and no one seemed to see him.' Her voice heavy with self-recrimination, she added, 'No one except me!'

'I thought we had it all worked out. I thought these people were being brainwashed, but the media, all this…' Jack waved a hand at the silent TV. 'They need it. They need to know – to *see* – what's happening, what's real, all the time or else… else…'

'They start to imagine,' said Rose numbly. 'It happened before as well. This morning, I saw… I was seeing things. I did think… I dunno, but I wondered if it could be to do with Static. I saw Static, Jack.'

'Domnic said this Gryden guy hadn't been around too long – not as long as the fiction ban – but I guess he could…'

He was distracted by the TV. It was showing live footage of what a subtitled reporter referred to as a 'fiction riot'. The rioters appeared to be few in number and unarmed – unlike the police, who were laying into them with guns and shock batons. The disturbance was quickly quelled and the subtitled reporter warned that this would be the fate of all those who chose to believe in Hal Gryden's warped fantasies.

'I guess they ran out of stories about traffic lights and car-park spaces,' said Rose.

Jack had made up his mind. 'What they're doing here,' he said, 'it's wrong. I don't care if the inmates in this place *are* sick, if fiction is driving them nuts or what – what they did to you, what they tried to do to me, it's just… it's wrong.'

'So let's stop it.'

They looked at each other and their faces broke out into simultaneous grins.

Jack produced the key cards again and handed one of them to Rose. 'You up to this?'

'Still a bit stiff down the left side, but it's wearing off.'

'You take this floor, I'll do the one above. First inmate I find who's halfway sane, I'll give 'em the third card, they can start on the third floor. The cops think they've got trouble now? Let's show 'em what the word really means!'

# FOURTEEN

It was back. The same monster, at the foot of her bed again. Kimmi knew all too well its fierce red eyes and its big black mouth and the tufts of blue hair that sprouted from its bottom lip. She had backed away from it as far as she could, to where the bed met the wall at the pillow end. She was scrunched into the corner, sobbing, terrified that the monster would drag her back to that place.

Then it sprang for her, and she screamed and woke, sitting bolt upright in her bed.

She was cold with sweat, her heart racing, and she wanted to cry. She hadn't had the dream for so long – but no matter how many times she told herself she was over it, how many pills she took, it always returned. Always as real as the first time. And in that dream, she was no longer the confident and respected Inspector Waller, the identity she had built for herself – she was helpless little Kimmi Waller again.

The Doctor. It was his fault. He had wormed his way through her protective shell to expose the frightened child beneath.

All she could do was try not to think about it.

It was late afternoon. A few more hours before she went back on duty. She had been on late shift for as long as she could remember, ever since she'd joined up. She liked it that way. She preferred to go to sleep, and to wake, with daylight in her eyes and the sound of traffic in her ears. During the day, she could hear people talking on the street and moving in the flats to each side of hers, and above and below. During the day, she didn't feel so lonely.

It was harder to keep out the dream at night.

She fixed herself a light snack from a recipe she had found in a magazine. She pottered about the flat she had decorated alone to an approved colour scheme. She ignored the snuffling of the monster in the bedroom, because she knew it was fictional. She did a bit of cleaning, just killing time, keeping herself busy.

She was needed more during the night. It was during the night that other people had bad dreams.

Her newspaper arrived at about half past five and she was shocked to discover how much the world had changed in her short absence.

The newsreader on 8 News didn't know which incident to report first. Her delivery was breathless, her eyes wide and staring, and it was clear to Waller that she was on the verge of going fantasy crazy herself.

There had been rioting, looting, thefts, even a couple of murders. The newsreader was at pains to point out that the outbreaks were isolated, that most of the streets were still safe – but she was obliged to confess that such an explosion of crime was unprecedented.

Waller knew immediately who was to blame.

Damn Steel! He had to be stretched to the limit – why hadn't he called her? So what if the law said she had to have a minimum of eight hours between shifts?

She grimaced and chased the thought away. The law was factual. To break it was tantamount to lying; like saying the law wasn't right, that it wasn't there for everybody's protection.

And yet, still…

Her black helmet stared at her from its perch on the back of a chair, like the blank face of a stranger. Like the person she became when she wore it.

There was a burglary in progress in Sector Nine-Two-Delta-One. In Sector Four-One-Beta, there had been a rash of graffiti. In Sector Five-Seven-Gamma-Five, some sociopath was pushing custard pies into people's faces and running away.

The newsreaders on every channel agreed. It was Hal Gryden's fault.

Waller thought long and hard before, slowly, almost in a trance, she knelt in front of her TV screen. She flipped open the concealed panel in the wall beside it and reached for the tuning controls. Know your enemy, she thought. It may be dangerous, but at least it would be the truth.

She found it in seconds. Static. She knew Hal Gryden's face, even though she had never seen it before. Dark eyes, bald head, a scar running the length of one cheek, every inch the villain. Just as she had always imagined him.

He was ranting in a voice that cut through Waller like a blade of ice:

*− time has come at last, my loyal, brainwashed disciples. Time to rise up against authority, to drag this world down into chaos. Forget the rights of the many − it's time to exercise your rights. Time to follow your dreams, even if it means war!*

She stabbed at the 'off' switch with a shudder, fearing that if she heard any more she'd be dragged back into that madness.

She had crossed the room before she knew it, started pulling on her uniform, feeling the weight of the micro-motors beneath the black mesh. She checked the power pack in her gun, thumbed on the vidcom on her wrist and hesitated.

The blank helmet seemed to be mocking her, as if it had always known she would give in. But the vidcom was picking up random messages from cops across the sector.

'– *too many of them* –'

'– *can't hold the line* –'

'– *crazy out here* –'

'– *need urgent backup* –'

And her choice was made.

She picked up her bike from the parking garage and lowered the helmet onto her head, becoming that person again. She slapped the vidcom into its slot on the dashboard and it flared into life almost immediately.

'*Waller,*' said Steel, his features grim but reassuring as always. '*We need you.*'

'I know,' she said.

Steel inspected her over the link, seeing that she was in uniform and ready to go. He condoned her decision with the merest hint of a nod. '*40th and 1090th,*' he said in his usual businesslike tone. '*Reports of a group of fiction geeks taking part in a role-playing game right out in the street.*'

'The scum!'

'You have to stop it, Waller. It's only a small step from role-playing games to devil worship.'

'Don't worry, Steel, I'm on it.'

She roared out onto the roadway.

The city looked as it always had, packed with people driving or trudging from work to home and vice versa. Today, though, there was a difference in the air. Something under the surface. Waller wondered how many of the people she could see were viewers of Static, followers of Hal Gryden. How many were harbouring fictional thoughts, just waiting until she was out of sight or until they could pluck up the courage to act on them.

Gryden had spoken the truth about one thing. Her world was at war.

And with that thought came the proof of it: an explosion, shaking the roadway beneath her jets, sending a column of smoke up into the air.

She hadn't imagined it. Other people had heard it, felt it, too. They were falling against each other, afraid.

It was her job to save them.

Waller turned her bike around with a screech, the rogue role-players forgotten.

She headed for the source of the disturbance.

By the time she got there, the fire brigade had arrived and were hovering on their anti-gravity platforms, spraying foam through the flame-licked windows of an office block. The fire seemed to have engulfed three floors and workers were stumbling from the building's main entrance doors below, coughing and spluttering, faces blackened by soot.

Passers-by were panicking, screaming, trying to run, and Waller could see no obvious culprit for the bombing. She intercepted a few people, tried to question them, but it was like Arno Finch's bank siege all over again. They had witnessed something outside their experience, something for which they hadn't been prepared, and their minds were racing, imagining.

Frustration welled up inside her, and before she knew what she was doing, she was firing her gun into the air, yelling for calm. 'I am an officer of the law and you will answer my questions!' She only made things worse.

Trapped at the centre of a storm of hysteria, Kimmi Waller had never felt so helpless.

And then her eyes alighted on an info-screen on the side of a hypermarket, and it all seemed unimportant.

The pictures were innocuous enough: just shots of the outside of the Big White House. But the subtitles told a terrible story:

*– coming in of a disturbance at the Home for the Cognitively Disconnected. We spoke to a doctor who*

*managed to escape the building as the trouble*
*started. He told us that many of the home's patients*
*had been released from their secure rooms and were*
*wreaking havoc. A police spokesperson has assured 8*
*News that the situation is in hand and that there is*
*no call for speculation. This is only the latest in a*
*series —*

It made a chilling sense. The Big White House. Where else would Gryden find so many misguided converts to his evil cause? What other building was such a great symbol of the laws he hated? On what other battlefield would he draw so much of the attention he obviously craved?

Everything else was a distraction. The Big White House was where this war would be won or lost.

It was three sectors away – strictly speaking, outside Waller's jurisdiction.

On the bike, she could be there in about twenty minutes.

It was getting dark as she rode up to the Big White House, but the lighting units of a dozen news crews provided a bubble of illumination on the street in front of it. There were police bikes all over the roadway, but not as many as she might have expected. Evidently Gryden's tactics were working and too many cops were tied up with his followers elsewhere.

No one seemed to know what to do. The rules didn't cover a situation like this, because it had been considered inconceivable to the people who had drawn them up.

A number of heated arguments had broken out, everyone shouting over each other. Waller only hoped that the channels receiving this footage were responsible enough not to broadcast it. The last thing the people needed right now was to see their guardians, their authority figures, squabbling like infants.

She strode through the sea of uniforms, exuding authority, silencing angry voices in her wake. She picked on a short, wiry constable who was screaming at the man in front of him, emphasising his point by stabbing a forefinger into his chest.

'You!' she barked. 'Who's in charge here?'

He turned to face her, took in the pips on her shoulder and jerked to attention. 'You are, ma'am. By my reckoning, you're the most senior officer present.'

And now everybody had fallen silent and was looking at her. Waiting for her instructions. And Waller had no idea what to say, because she had never been in charge of an operation like this. There had never *been* an operation like this.

She had dreamed of this moment, though. Guilty, secret dreams, yes, but ones in which she had risen to just such a momentous challenge. The chance to end Hal Gryden's threat once and for all.

Her vidcom buzzed and she heard Steel's voice from her wrist: *'I heard everything, Waller, and he's right. You're the highest-ranking officer at the scene. You have to do this. You* can *do this.'*

'Why haven't we gone in yet?' she asked.

'Doors are barricaded,' one of the officers answered.

'Then break them down!'

'He's taken hostages, ma'am.'

'"He"?'

'The ringleader. Calls himself Captain Jack.'

And then there was only the moment and the orders tripped easily off Waller's tongue: orders that the escapees from the Big White House be questioned again, that the records of the chief instigators be pulled, that riot equipment be requisitioned and that someone get her a vidphone link to this 'Captain Jack'.

A camera orb was pushed into her face and she gave a terse but reassuring statement to the watching world.

Then a sergeant came running up to her and pressed a phone into her hand. 'We've made contact, ma'am.'

Waller glanced at the image on the phone's screen. Pretty boy, she thought dismissively. Then she took another look and had the same thought again, only more warmly this time.

She blinked and pulled herself together. 'All right, pal,' she growled, 'no fiction. Just tell me what it takes to end this.'

Captain Jack's response was equally brusque. '*A change in the law. Most of the people in here have done nothing wrong. Yeah, some of them are sick, and they need treatment – but not the sort that gets dished out here. And the rest just need to be left to get on with it, not persecuted for reading a book or listening to a good story or telling someone they look nice today when they don't.*'

'You're asking the impossible,' said Waller. 'If you weren't fantasy crazy, you'd know that. The law doesn't change, ever.'

'*Time it did,*' said Jack. '*If you can't do it, find someone who can. You know we've got hostages.*'

'That a threat?'

'*It's a statement of fact, just how you like it.*'

'Is Hal Gryden in there? I want to speak to Hal Gryden.'

'*Never met the guy. Look, I hate negotiating by phone. It's so impersonal. You wanna have dinner? We got food in the kitchens here – you just bring the wine and the candles. Oh, and keep the uniform. It's sexy!*'

And then, with a cheeky wink, Captain Jack cut off the connection, leaving Waller flustered and unsure how to react.

If he'd asked for money or a fast car, she could have stalled him. As it was, she had no idea – no idea at all

– how she could have begun to address his demands even if she'd wanted to.

'Let me talk to him.'

The voice sent a chill down her spine. She turned, to find herself – as expected – looking into a pair of intense blue eyes: eyes that could stare through her helmet visor, right into her childlike soul.

'Let me talk to him,' repeated the Doctor.

'He hung up.'

'I know. I meant I could go into the building.'

'No chance. I couldn't guarantee your safety.'

'He won't hurt me.'

'He's fantasy crazy. You don't know what he'll do.'

'Hero complex. Thinks he's saving the world. I know the type. And he wants publicity. I work for a TV channel, remember?'

'I didn't know that!'

The interjection came from a sandy-haired kid with a floppy fringe. Waller hadn't noticed him before, standing at the Doctor's elbow.

The Doctor smiled tightly and laid an arm across the kid's shoulders. 'New research assistant. Still training him up. So, what do you say? Do I get to report on the news story of the century? Inspector Waller's triumphant retaking of the Big White House, as told from the inside?' He let go of the kid and leaned in closer to Waller, lowering his voice. 'I could help you, you know. Take a vidphone in there, find a quiet corner, give you a call, let you know what's happening, how the land lies, that kind of thing.'

He certainly made the idea sound appealing – and it wasn't as if Waller had a better one. 'So I just let you in there?' she said numbly.

'Yeah.'

'You and your… assistant?'

The Doctor glanced at the kid as if he had forgotten he was there, then shrugged. 'Yeah, I s'pose so.'

'And if it all goes wrong, if they kill you…'

'Then you warned me. You were truthful. No one could blame you.'

Waller looked at the cops around her, feeling the weight of their expectations. In the end, she just knew she had to make a decision, give an order, or lose all their respect. In the end, she had no choice.

'As soon as you can,' she said sternly, 'you call the police emergency number. They'll route you straight through to my vidcom.'

'Got it,' said the Doctor.

And he was already halfway to the gates, the kid at his heels.

'Wait! Aren't you taking a camera in with you?'

He hesitated, turned and patted his pockets as if expecting to find just such a device in one of them. Then, brightly, he called back, 'I'll improvise!'

And he was off again.

'Remember,' Waller called after him, because she

wanted to regain that fleeting feeling she had had before he'd turned up: the feeling that she was actually in control. 'I'm waiting for that call!'

But the Doctor didn't answer her.

# FIFTEEN

'Situation?' The Doctor strode through the empty panelled passageways of the ground floor of the Big White House, Captain Jack by his side, Domnic struggling to keep up with them both.

'The building is in rebel hands,' reported Jack, all clipped and efficient. 'We released all the patients, apart from those in the secure cells on the top floor of the central block. Our forces number about 500. Discounting those who are deluded to the point of uselessness or zoned out on drugs or who just don't want to fight, that number comes down to about 220.'

'Hostages?'

'Sixty-three. The orderlies here are used to outnumbering the patients. We took 'em by surprise. Some ran. The rest we locked in the fourth-floor dorms.'

'Defences?'

'We got our most rational guys watching the ground-floor doors and windows, but they won't be so easy to hold. The rest of us are based up on Three. The only ways up are the lifts and two staircases. We're doing the best we can, but we're ill-equipped and ill-prepared. Frankly, we're relying on the hostages to keep the cops at bay. We wouldn't hurt them, but they don't know that.'

Two patients were manning a lift each, keeping them down here with their doors open in case of need. The Doctor noted that the other two lifts were similarly locked on the third and fourth floors respectively.

'Plan?' he prompted, as they rode upwards.

'Ah. That's where we're winging it a little. Primary aim is to gather intel, find out who or what is responsible for the anti-fiction laws. I'm guessing that, if we kick up enough of a fuss here, they'll come to us.'

'They already have,' the Doctor murmured.

The lift reached its destination with a ping and the doors rattled open to reveal two more pyjama-clad sentries. The Doctor recognised Arno Finch, who acknowledged him with a weak smile as he passed and ventured uncertainly, 'I'm doing it. I'm doing what you said, Doctor. Making a real difference. Aren't I?'

He had only one question left, but it was the most important one.

'And Rose?'

The third floor was abuzz with activity.

People were standing up beds to block windows, breaking up furniture to use as weapons, or just running around, caught up in the excitement and probably dreaming that they were anywhere else but here. One woman was in tears, believing the building to be under attack from bomber planes. She was led gently into a dorm and encouraged to have a lie-down.

Rose was a few doors away, huddled up on a bed in the dark. The TV screen in her room had been smashed. She greeted the Doctor with a smile and a 'Hi', but neither reached as far as her eyes.

He was with her in two strides, assuring her that he was who he appeared to be and that she was safe now.

'You found the monsters, then?' she asked, forcing herself to sound cheerful but not quite succeeding.

'Oh yeah.' He tapped a forefinger against her temple. 'They're in here.'

Rose flushed. 'What's that s'posed to mean?'

The Doctor moved the finger to his own head. 'They're in here too. Micro-organisms in the air of this world. The settlers' equipment isn't sensitive enough to detect them and it's been a long time since they looked anyway.'

'Which means… what? We're all just breathing 'em in?'

The Doctor grinned. 'Yeah. Hold on, here comes the science bit. These organisms feed off electrical activity in the atmosphere. They were probably quite happy till human beings came here and offered them something a bit tastier.'

'You mean our… brains? They're eating our brains?'

'Er, not quite. Just absorbing their neuroelectro-chemical signals. The right side of the adult human brain has the best flavour, apparently. It's like sugar to them. They've become quite the addicts, started colonising wholesale in there.' He tapped Rose's temple again. 'Trouble is, too much right-brain activity – dreams, for example – and they get bloated. The surplus impulses are reflected back where they came from, creating a feedback loop.' He was twirling his fingers in a hopeless attempt to demonstrate. 'The dreamer finds his dreams amplified over and over again until the right brain reacts to them as if they're real and communicates that information –' he clasped his hands together and described an arc through the air – 'to the left brain.'

'Left brain,' repeated Rose, still not quite following.

'Yeah. Logic, reasoning, language, all that stuff. And memory.'

'So that's why they... they kind of half froze my brain...'

'So you couldn't dream, yeah.'

'All the muscles down my left-hand side...'

'Right side of the brain controls the left side of the body.'

'But you can make it better – can't you?'

'Once we get to the TARDIS, yeah. I can flush the micro-organisms right out of your system. Till then...'

Rose's face fell.

'You can get through this!' said the Doctor. 'If the people of this world can learn to live with it – well, most of the time – I know you can. You know what the monsters are now, Rose. You can fight them.'

'Did... did Jack tell you...'

'That you tried to break into the Big White House cos you thought I told you to? Nope, didn't need to. I read your note at the hotel.'

Rose avoided his gaze. 'You must think I'm pretty thick.'

'Not your fault.'

'Seeing things that aren't there, though.'

'Not your fault.'

'And it's like... like even after – after I knew what was wrong with me, yeah, I kept... We were letting the patients out, and the orderlies didn't know what had hit them. I thought they were gonna tear some of 'em apart. There were people running and screaming and fighting, and it was like… I didn't know how much of it was real and how much…'

'Not your fault.'

'Doctor… You know last night, in the café… when I said you were "mental"…'

'I know,' he said gently. 'Tell me something: was I clever?'

The question threw Rose. 'Eh?'

'When I brought you here. Was I clever?'

'You weren't… I mean, *he* wasn't…'

'Real. I know, yeah. But was I clever? That version of me, in your head – was I resourceful and witty and charming and handsome?'

For the first time, a hint of a smile – a genuine smile – broke through her awkwardness. 'Bit full of yourself, aren't you?'

'Bit full of *yourself*.'

'I don't get it.'

'Pat yourself on the back, Rose Tyler – cos all that cleverness and resourcefulness and that wit and that charm, it came from inside you.'

'And the handsome?'

'Well…' said the Doctor, with a modest shrug.

And Rose remembered how to laugh.

Cal Tyko looked up as the Doctor entered his dorm. Recognition flickered in his eyes and was joined by hope – until he saw the two patients standing guard at his visitor's shoulder, and fear took over.

He scrambled off the bed and backed up to the wall, his eyes wide. The Doctor wondered what nightmares he was seeing.

'Cal Tyko,' he said with a tight smile. 'Got something for you.'

'What… what are you going to do to me?' gasped Tyko, trembling, finding his voice at last.

'What, you don't wanna take your own medicine? It's for your own good. You look fantasy crazy to me. Don't you want to get better?'

'I was just… just doing my job. Just trying to help people.'

'Yeah, me and you both, mate.' The Doctor found a crumpled piece of paper in his pocket and threw it at Tyko with contempt. 'Difference is, I don't lobotomise them in the process. Here! A few ideas about what's causing your problem. The rest's up to you. Unless you want things to stay like this for ever.'

'You're asking me to… to…'

'To take a leap of faith, yeah. Scary, isn't it!'

Then the Doctor turned and breezed out, not looking back to see if Tyko had reached for the balled-up paper.

He had a great deal more still to do.

At the far end of the third floor from the lifts, the

Doctor found an office like the one in which Tyko had left him and Waller that morning: desk, chairs, computer, screens over two walls, no windows. It had been overrun by inmates, but he quickly shooed them out.

He sat at the computer, took a few seconds to familiarise himself with its operating system, then opened its Ethernet connection. Within minutes, he had found his way through several backdoors and three firewalls to a server that had not been used for decades and yet, as he'd hoped, had never actually been dismantled. A server that had belonged to the old government.

'Um... Doctor?'

He'd been aware of Domnic's presence for a while; he had just been ignoring him. His eyes remained fixed on the monitor, his fingers a blur on the keyboard.

'These... these micro-organisms. You said they'd come back.'

'Yeah. They're already swimming up your nose, through your mouth, down your ears. Won't be long before there are enough of them in your brain to start the delusions all over again.'

'But you can drive them out again, right?'

'Could. Won't be here.'

'I... see.' Domnic sounded disappointed, but he made no move to leave.

For a minute or so there was silence. Then the Doctor gave up his work in exasperation. 'There's something else, isn't there? There's always something else.'

'I… I've been watching TV in one of the patients' dorms.'

'Well, good for you,' he said scathingly. 'Life pretty much back to normal for you already, eh?'

'I was looking for Static. I thought… you know, with everything going on, I thought it'd still be… I can't find it, Doctor. I can't find it on any frequency.'

'Oh, is that all?' said the Doctor. 'Doesn't exist.'

Domnic's jaw trembled. 'You… you mean…'

'Static. Hal Gryden. All fiction. Any more questions?'

'How…'

He came into the room proper and sank into the spare chair. He looked shell-shocked and it occurred to the Doctor that he'd been a bit brusque. He'd related the bare facts without considering the effect they might have. Domnic had suspected the truth already – but still, its confirmation had dashed his hopes. And on Colony World 4378976.Delta-Four, hope was hard enough to come by.

'I saw you in the hotel room, remember?' he said, more kindly. 'You said you were watching Static. You were more right than you knew.'

'Then the revolution, everything he said… All lies.

Nothing's gonna change.'

'Yeah, it will. Gryden might not be real, but he's the next best thing. He's an urban legend. Everyone believes in him and on this world that *makes* him real. Even the newspapers and the TV news are talking about him. You saw the info-screens on our way in here. Your revolution's started, with or without its figurehead.'

'Fantastic!'

'No,' said the Doctor, 'not "fantastic". Very, very far from "fantastic" – cos this world doesn't need a revolution. There's no one to revolt against. All you can do is tear yourselves apart and, believe me, that ball's already started to roll. Soon, no one will be able to stop it. If I can't find a way to save this world pronto, there won't be much of a world left to save.'

It took Domnic some time to come up with a reaction to that, and then all he could manage was, 'Oh.'

'Camera,' said the Doctor abruptly. Apparently, that wasn't enough, so he explained, 'I need a video camera. There are plenty around. In every dorm, behind the telly. Or the ones in the corridors might be easier to get hold of. Get a couple of the patients to help you. They're used to obeying anyone who shows the slightest authority.'

He'd already returned to his work when he realised that Domnic was still sitting there dumbly – and that maybe even 'the slightest authority' was too much to ask of him. 'Go and see Captain Jack,' he sighed. 'He'll find a few pairs of hands for you. Go on, then, quick as you like!'

The camera was set up on a makeshift tripod constructed from three chairs, its lens trained on the desk. Its innards were hanging out, trailing wires to the computer, and in the middle of this lash-up sat the Doctor's sonic screwdriver, glowing with blue light. The Doctor himself was running from computer to camera to screwdriver, checking connections, taking readings here, making adjustments there – and explaining his plan to the audience he had somehow acquired.

'Best way to save this world,' he said, 'is to use its most powerful weapon.'

'What's that?' asked Domnic.

'It's the media, isn't it?' said Rose. 'The telly.'

'Gold star,' said the Doctor, taking her by the shoulders and moving her gently but firmly out of his way. 'There are thirty-six TV channels serving this planet, but they all bounce their signals off the same satellite – which I've just located. Amazing what you can find on the Net these days.'

Jack frowned. 'You mean to cut in on *all* those channels?'

'No point in doing half a job.'

Rose grinned as she clarified matters to the watching patients: 'He's seen this on *Batman*. It's how the villains always deliver their ransom demands to Gotham City.'

'This part of the building – this block – it's steel-reinforced concrete,' Jack mused. 'You could use its framework as an aerial.'

'Yup.'

'But to blanket all frequencies, you'd have to send a broad-spectrum transmission.'

'Yup.'

'Does the sonic screwdriver have enough power for that?'

'Nope.'

'No?' echoed Domnic in dismay.

The Doctor dropped into his chair at the computer and started typing again. 'Had a better idea. When this world had a government, they set up an emergency distress channel – overrides the signals to all other channels in the event of a global disaster: riots, wars, invasions, monsters, that kind of thing.'

Jack nodded in admiration. 'So you crack the frequency of the government distress signal, then we only need a narrowband transmission to activate the override.'

'And you can do that?' asked Domnic.

'It's protected by a series of pass codes,' said the Doctor, 'but I've knocked together a little program that should see to that in about…' He smiled as the computer pinged and the screen lit up with the data he needed.

'So, you're gonna talk to the world,' said Rose. 'What are you gonna say?'

'Gonna give them what they need,' said the Doctor. 'A hero.' Catching Rose's smirk and raised eyebrow, he added, 'I don't mean me. Hal Gryden. These people created him because they needed somebody. Least I can do is make him real for them – I mean *really* real – make their dreams come true.'

'I don't get it,' said Rose. 'You're gonna – what? – pretend to be Gryden yourself?'

'And let everyone see him,' realised Jack. 'Or at least let them *think* they've seen him. Don't you get it, Rose? Then, when they think about Gryden, they won't be imagining him – they'll be *remembering* the Doctor.'

'Using the left hemispheres of their brains instead of the right,' ventured Rose, her brow furrowing as she remembered what the Doctor had told her.

'Best way to stop someone dreaming is to make their dreams come true,' said the Doctor. 'Should calm things down for a while. One problem.'

'As always,' said Rose cheerfully.

'Inspector Waller won't be too chuffed about this.'

'We've still got the hostages,' Jack pointed out.

'Yeah, but the way the cops see it, ideas are more

dangerous than any physical threat – and we'll be spreading ideas like mad. Soon as I start my speech – soon as they see what I'm doing, and they will, on the info-screens outside, just like the rioters will – they're gonna storm this building. Not much I can do about that. You'll just have to be ready, all of you.'

'We're ready,' said Jack.

'No, we're not!' said Rose.

'As we're ever gonna be,' Jack amended. 'We can't hold them back, but we can buy you, say, ten minutes.'

'Should be enough. I'll need a camera person. Volunteers?'

One of the patients raised a tentative hand.

'Fine,' said the Doctor. He clapped his hands together, took a deep breath and met the eyes of each of the onlookers in turn. 'Well, then,' he said softly, 'I think it's time to man the barricades!'

# SIXTEEN

There was a mattress blocking the barred window of the empty dorm, bolstered by a bed and a chest of drawers.

Rose peeled back the edge of it and looked out cautiously across the Big White House's concreted grounds. From up here, she could see over the perimeter wall to where the road was swarming with black uniforms. More police bikes were arriving all the time – and as she watched a black truck pulled up on the edge of her field of vision and cops started to unload equipment through its back doors.

She hated this part: when the plan was made and the risks spelled out, but before everything had kicked off. And this time it was worse, because she knew she couldn't let herself think about what was to come.

It was the same for everyone, of course. She could

feel their anticipation, their fear, like a physical force. She was comforted by the weight of the table leg in her hand.

So long as she didn't think about what the cops might be carrying.

The Doctor had never pretended he could save her from everything. Rose didn't even want him to.

As if she hadn't read his expression when he'd asked for a camera person, caught the flicker of his eyes towards her. He had to know by now that she wouldn't have taken him up on his offer, his way off the front line. He had still had to make it.

She glanced at the TV screen on the wall. It was showing fires and riots and looting; people throwing concrete blocks at cops and even at the cameras. Rose could hardly believe she was looking at the same streets she had walked just a few hours ago. Everything had spun out of control so fast. It hardly seemed real.

One major channel, apparently, had been taken off-air when its studios had been invaded. A police spokesperson was urging the public to remain calm, to stay in their homes – until he broke down in tears and confessed to the world that there was nothing he could do, that his force was outnumbered and that, contrary to his previous statements, the truth was that everyone was going to die.

The programme's editors cut back to a stunned

newsreader who fiddled with her data pad and tried to think of something to say.

She was spared the effort as her image suddenly crackled and died. There was a brief burst of static, then a new picture wobbled uncertainly into view.

The Doctor was out of focus at first, visible only from the neck down. He rushed forward until his navy-blue shirt filled the screen. He seemed to be having a row with the patient behind the camera; Rose cranked the volume up and heard muffled voices. Blurred fingers clashed over the lens. Then the Doctor's face dropped into view, ridiculously huge, his nostrils gaping like caverns. He blinked, grinned and backed away until he was perched on his desk, now perfectly framed.

'*Um, yeah, hi,*' he said – and he smiled again, self-consciously.

Come on, Doctor, thought Rose, pull it together!

'*You're watching Static,*' said the Doctor, playing with his hands, '*broadcasting on all frequencies for… for as long as we can. I think you all know me, though I might not look quite as you imagined.*'

Rose looked out of the window again. From here she could see an info-screen and the edge of another out in the street, and they were both displaying the Doctor's image. His words were even subtitled; presumably, that was automatic.

She wasn't at all surprised, then, to see that a

change had come over the cops. Most of them had just been milling about, but now they all moved with a purpose. Some of them were returning to their bikes, while others…

… most of them were surging through the front gates…

'They're coming!' yelled Rose, racing out of the dorm into the corridor, careful to lock the door behind her. 'The cops are coming!'

The warning was echoed from six other doors and was greeted by agitated murmurs all the way up to the stairs.

An elderly woman dropped the kitchen knife she'd been carrying and fell to her knees. She was laughing hysterically, but crying too. 'You're finished now, you fiction geeks!' she wailed. 'You're headed for a real big dose of reality. You just wait till they get you back in the operating theatres, you just wait!'

And, over the racket, Rose could just make out the Doctor's voice: *'I'm Hal Gryden – and I've got something important to tell you.'*

The shouting began on the ground floor.

Rose's stomach tightened at the sound. There were only a few people down there. Their job was to hold the doors as long as they could, then fall back to the stairs. At best, they would buy seconds – but even seconds counted.

Only a few people. But Captain Jack was one of them.

Rose and the rest of the third-floor army were crowded into the space in front of the lifts, the more eager of them spilling out onto the stairs with their makeshift weapons. They were listening and waiting, in a silence so heavy that it could almost have suffocated her.

Domnic was beside her. He had slipped through the crowd, trying to make it look like a coincidence that he'd ended up just here. She smiled at him and he smiled back weakly, struggling to be brave.

Rose was picturing Jack in the thick of the fight downstairs, giving orders, dispensing jokes and innuendo to keep up the morale of his troops. Living up to a rank that – she was almost certain – he had bestowed upon himself.

They'd never get the better of him. She believed in him.

But what if something went wrong?

'*I messed up,*' the Doctor was broadcasting, more confident now, getting into his role. '*I've been telling you that fiction's good, and I stand by that. But I got one thing wrong. I was treating the symptoms, ignoring the cause.*'

Two of the four lifts began to rise. They rumbled past her floor, on their way to the fifth: a diversion, to make the cops think the Doctor was all the way up there.

She heard footsteps on the stairs. If everything was

going according to plan, then Jack and a few others would be coming this way.

The lifts came to an abrupt halt, all at once, between the fourth and fifth floors. Jack had expected that, though. He'd known the cops would have an override device and he had taken precautions.

Fighting had broken out on the stairs, two floors down. Rose could hear booted footsteps and gunshots and yells. The cops must have run into the first-floor defenders: a smaller force than was stationed up here, but their role was just as vital.

The Doctor was using the whole of this five-storey block as his aerial. That would make it impossible to pinpoint his signal to a single room – and the cops would be desperate to find it. Jack had reckoned they'd split their forces, try to search every floor at once. The longer they could be held up on the first, second and fifth floors, the more time the Doctor would have.

The fourth floor was reserved for the hostages and for those patients who couldn't or did not wish to fight. They would surrender as soon as the first uniform appeared.

The lifts were heading downwards, passing the third floor again. Rose swallowed anxiously. If the cops gained control over them…

But then, with a judder and a terrible screeching,

they ground to a halt. The patients on the top floor had followed their instructions and jammed the gears.

The fighting was still coming closer, though.

It sounded as if the cops had reached the second floor, too soon. That meant they were already wading through the patients on the first, searching rooms, narrowing down the location of their primary target.

*'There's no need to fight, no point. It's not what I wanted. I wanted you to dream of building, not of tearing things down.'*

Jack came barrelling out of the stairwell and Rose's heart leaped at the sight of him. He was flushed with excitement. A small bruise grazed his temple and his grey jumpsuit had a tear down one sleeve.

'OK,' he cried, 'looks like we're up. Good luck, everyone!'

And after that, there was no time for worries any more.

It looked like a solid force of black, surging towards her.

The police came charging up the stairs, preceded by a barrage of blue blaster fire. The defenders were tackling them, hitting them, but their helmets and padded armour absorbed most of the blows, and they were hardly slowed at all.

A couple of cops fell, but their colleagues didn't care. They just trampled over them, as they trampled over their foes, climbing with single-minded purpose.

Rose was doing her best, but the people around her were inexperienced, half of them panicking, some trying to back out of the stairwell and run. She was pushed this way and that, just trying to find the room to swing her weapon. A blue ball of energy fizzed past her hip, to hit a young kid squarely in the stomach, flooring him.

Jack had gone into battle ahead of her. He was somewhere further down the stairs and she thought he must have been overrun because she couldn't see him.

And then a cop was reaching for her, planting a gloved hand in her face, trying to push her over. She braced herself against two people behind her and kicked as hard as she could at his stomach. He was winded, doubled up, and Rose brought her table leg down hard. The cop's helmet rang with the impact, the vibrations rattling the bones of Rose's hands. The cop almost fell, but was caught by two of his colleagues behind him. Rose wrestled with him, tried to snatch the gun from his hand, but he held on to it with all his strength. Still, the two of them were effectively blocking the stairwell – until the cop recovered his wits and gave Rose a push that sent her reeling.

Total time gained for the Doctor: about ten seconds.

'Rose! Rose!'

Someone was screaming her name. Rose realised that she had fallen back almost as far as the third-floor entrance. She fought her way out to Domnic and her eyes followed the direction of his pointing, trembling finger.

She was back in front of the lifts. From here, white corridors stretched in three directions: one straight ahead, leading to a T-junction, the other two left and right, meeting windows at the points at which they turned away. The windows had been barricaded, of course, as well as the defenders had been able to manage. But the barricade to the left was shaking, falling apart, and Rose could see a shadow behind it and hear, even over the clamour on the stairs, the whine of hoverjets.

She ran for the window, intending to shore up the last upended bed.

She was too late.

A bright light smacked her in the eyes and, when her vision cleared, there was a cop climbing through the window frame, through shattered glass, pushing chests of drawers and other clutter out of his way.

And another waiting to follow him, balanced on a floating disc outside.

And behind them, a third cop on a police bike, its engines straining to keep it this high, its searchlight glaring.

Rose ran at the first of the invaders, whirling her

table leg, yelling to Domnic to help her. She met the cop before he could get into the building proper, caught him still straddling the window sill. She struggled to push him back out, trying not to think about whether he was padded well enough to survive a three-storey drop. One of his mates would catch him, wouldn't they?

She was attempting to get his gun, but, like the cop on the stairs, he was too strong – and Rose remembered what Jack had said about micro-motors in their uniforms. Still, she almost had it – until she realised that the cop on the disc outside had drawn his own gun and was aiming…

She ducked, using the body of the cop in the window as a shield.

She realised that this gun didn't look like the others. It was bigger and silver.

And something whistled over Rose's head, to land with a plop in the corridor behind her.

Some sort of a gas bomb. It was releasing fumes. Thin, green fumes.

Her first thought was to grab it, to hurl it outside, but her opponent had a grip on her arm and he yanked her back, away from it. Her hands flew automatically to his neck and she felt a catch there… No time to think. She just popped it, pulled the helmet from the cop's head. His grip was released as he threw up his hands to stop her – but he was a fraction too slow and Rose staggered back out of his reach.

Something was scratching at her throat. Her eyes were filling up and she knew the gas was to blame. She put on the helmet, noting that she could see perfectly through the visor, which was opaque from the outside, and that she could breathe again, stale but untainted air.

The cop had extricated himself from the window frame and was running at her. Rose could see his face now, albeit cast into shadow by the searchlight behind it. It was surprisingly young, pale, still suffering from acne – and twisted in hatred for her. The gas was getting to the unmasked man – he was wheezing and spluttering. There were tears on his cheeks, but he still had his micro-motors, and he was driving her down onto her knees, raising his fist to strike.

And Domnic appeared from nowhere, through the green mist, screaming at the top of his lungs, cannoning into the cop – and Rose got just the briefest impression of his face, all screwed up and teary, both eyes tightly closed.

Domnic and the cop fell, and neither of them got up again.

They weren't the only ones.

Patients were running from the stairwell in all directions, desperate to escape from the gas, too many of them failing – and as Rose watched helplessly, the barricade fell from the window beyond them and another gas bomb flew into the building.

The first cops had emerged from the stairwell and they were tussling with the weakened defenders. Some had already got past them and were opening hatches in dorm doors, checking inside for the Doctor.

Rose almost didn't hear the hoverjets behind her until it was too late.

She whirled to see the police bike powering towards her, its rider hunching to fit through the broken window and yet still catching his shoulder painfully on the frame.

Rose's first instinct was to flatten herself against the wall. Her second was for the people in the mêlée behind her – patients and cops alike – and as the bike brushed past her, still accelerating, she grabbed its rider and was pulled along with him.

Her flailing foot found the back of the saddle, giving her leverage, but she had only a second. Faces were starting to turn towards them, people starting to scatter but only bumping into each other. What was this guy thinking?

She knew the answer to that one. Even cops could go fantasy crazy.

She reached over his shoulders, clamped her hands over his, squeezed hard, and just hoped that the brakes were in the handlebars of this thing.

The bike stopped abruptly, at the same time veering to the right and flipping onto its side, dashing Rose to the ground. The landing was softer than she had expected; she had thought she would be flung forwards, but somehow her momentum had been drained. Still, she was barely able to roll out of the way before bike and rider crashed into the space she had just vacated.

The cop was pinned down by his vehicle, shouting obscenities at her, and Rose scrambled away and climbed to her feet, feeling light-headed and wobbly.

She was back at the lifts, just about the only defender left standing. The patients had collapsed or fled, and the cops were moving systematically down the main corridor, continuing their search, nearing its end. What could she do? She couldn't fight them alone.

Then, suddenly, a set of lift doors shot open and she started…

… and then grinned at the sight of Captain Jack, suspended from the lift cable, gripping it with his ankles, one arm looped about it to press a handkerchief to his nose and mouth, the other holding a gun – trust him to have found one – with which he had evidently just shot out the doors' circuits. They were still smouldering.

She thought he wouldn't recognise her in the

helmet, through the green mist, but her clothes were obviously a dead giveaway.

'Not going so well, I take it?' said Jack cheerfully. He swung himself easily out of the shaft. 'How long's it been?'

Rose checked her watch and her heart sank. 'About seven minutes.'

'OK.' Jack was already running. 'Let's see if we can make eight at least.'

They took the corridor to the right because it was relatively empty. But the cops had gone the more direct route and were already battering down the door to the makeshift studio. Rose could hear the Doctor's voice on the far side, still talking, still calm. They were almost there, but the cops were running to meet them – dozens of them.

She wasn't afraid. She was determined. They had told the Doctor ten minutes and that was what he was going to get.

Jack had four paces on her and he sent a barrage of blaster fire the cops' way, then ploughed into them. He fought brilliantly – he could have matched any four of his opponents, maybe more – but there were just too many of them.

And the door splintered open.

Rose had eyes for only that, had thoughts for only the Doctor. In that moment, nothing else mattered to her except that she get to that door.

And somehow she did, slipping between the cops in her path, expecting to feel their hands on her collar; but they were surprised by her speed and her dexterity, and too busy with Jack.

And she raced into the small office, where a cop with pips on her shoulder and a uniform a bit too large for her was levelling a gun at the Doctor, who had stopped talking and was raising his hands.

'I trusted you,' spat the cop, 'and you were *him* all along. You lied to me!'

And Rose leaped onto her shoulders…

… to be thrown off with an almost casual shrug. She landed in a heap, found her arms pinned by two cops before she could stand again. And there were many more cops streaming into the room, more guns aimed at the Doctor's head, and his hapless volunteer was wide-eyed with fear as he was wrenched away from his camera.

'Turn it off!' the cop with the pips ordered.

'Why?' asked the Doctor.

'Because we've all heard enough of your lies!'

'But you're here now. Inspector Waller to the rescue. The world is watching you. Your chance to fix everything, set the record straight.'

Waller hesitated, gesturing to the cop who had picked up the camera to stay his hand for now. She was thinking about it.

'You can be the one who tells them the truth,' said the Doctor. 'The whole truth and nothing but the truth.'

And he smiled past the cops. At Rose.

# SEVENTEEN

**D**omnic had had a good day. A friend of his from the reading group had a friend who was setting up a publishing company. He was interested in fiction, maybe even comics, and he had agreed to look at some of Domnic's stories.

He'd made four phone sales at work, including one to a girl he hoped might become more than a customer. He'd told her that his company's windows were specially proofed against zombies and she had playfully called him a big liar.

'That obvious, huh?' he had said. 'I'm still new to it, you see – haven't had much practice.'

'Well, they're saying now that lying is good for a relationship,' she had rejoined.

At which point Domnic had let his dreams get the better of him. He'd blurted out a suggestion that they meet in the flesh to practise on each other some time

– and she had agreed.

Not tonight, though. Tonight was a special night.

Domnic had turned on the telly an hour early and was passing the time by surfing channels.

'– big match about to begin on 9 Sport, and for anyone who doesn't wish to speculate about the result, it was 2–1 to –'

'– of Sector Two-Three-Phi was delighted to be given a parking space closer to –'

'– viewers will decide whether Todd or Lucy – our two remaining contestants, who are about to emerge from the door behind me – gets to take home the Audience Shares grand prize: a starring role in their very own docu-drama!'

OK, so change didn't happen overnight.

But starting on Channel One tonight was a brand-new show – a drama, with a script and actors and everything – and its makers had promised to show viewers things from beyond their world.

Some people had already complained, before the show had even aired. They were saying it was too scary, too violent or offensive to their new-found religion. But they would be watching.

Everyone would be watching tonight – because this was something that, two months ago, they couldn't have imagined. Something different.

On 8 News, they were playing back the recording of the Doctor's confrontation with Inspector Waller again. Domnic had missed it the first time round, but he'd seen it often enough in the two months since.

'The only truth that needs telling here,' stormed Waller, 'is that you're fantasy crazy, the furthest gone I've ever seen! The people only have to look at you, Gryden. They only have to see what's happening out there.'

The Doctor shook his head. 'I didn't cause any of this. Pushed the process along, maybe, but…'

'It's your fault, you and your Static channel. The media is meant to inform, to educate. It tells us what's real, what we can believe. But you've corrupted it. You've used it to spread dissent and violence and fear!'

'Your people want change,' said the Doctor.

'Yeah,' piped up the voice of Rose Tyler from off-camera. 'And if you'd listened to what the Doctor was saying, you'd know –'

'I was calling for the violence to end. There's a better way.'

'Oh yeah, and don't we all know it!' spat Waller with distaste. 'Leave it to you, you'd have people dreaming as much as they like.'

'We all need dreams, Inspector Waller,' said the Doctor. 'Even you.'

Waller shook her head firmly. 'I'm happy with my real life, thank you. We've seen where your way leads. Everyone wanting different things, fighting for their own dreams.'

'Price you pay, I'm afraid. The freedom to hope, to imagine something better so you can make it real – worth it, believe me.'

Waller let out a hollow laugh. 'You're asking me to believe you?'

'Yeah. You're so concerned with the truth, aren't you?'

'It's all there is.'

'And what do your superiors think of that? Come on, Inspector Waller, why not talk to them? Find out what they think.'

'I don't have to. I know the law.'

'And the law never changes.'

'Right.'

'So prove it. Talk to them. Make me out to be a liar in front of the whole world.'

And then came Domnic's favourite part. The part where, after a moment's indecision, Waller brought up her wrist and spoke into her vidcom. The part where she asked somebody called Steel if he had heard, and requested instructions. The part where she nodded and grunted as if listening to someone, then thanked that invisible person and turned to the Doctor triumphantly.

'You see now, Gryden? Do you see who the liar is?'

The part where the camera zoomed in, to show that her vidcom was broken, blank, just the remnants of a shattered screen nestling in a mess of burnt-out circuitry.

'Yeah,' said the Doctor quietly. 'I think we all do.'

The other cops were shaken, unsure who to trust. They were wavering, some of them turning their guns on Waller herself.

'Course, I don't know the full story,' said the Doctor. 'I don't know where you got the uniform and the bike, but there's always a way if you want it badly enough. And of course, who'd question you? Who'd dare accuse a police officer of lying? Did the uniform come with the pips, by the way, or did you make them yourself, give yourself a promotion? How about the vidcom? Was it always broken, or did you break it yourself so you'd only hear the voices you wanted to hear?' He shifted his gaze to Waller's colleagues. 'Anyone else heard of this "Steel"? No? I wonder – if "Inspector" Waller got away with it this long, how many more impostors are there out there? How many in this room?'

Waller had dropped her gun. She looked as if the life had drained out of her. She was muttering something feebly. Sound technicians had worked hard to decipher the words, so that they could be subtitled. She was saying, 'I didn't mean to… I was only trying to put things right, fight the monsters…'

But the Doctor didn't let up. 'Ironic, isn't it, "Inspector", that you've spent so long denying other people their dreams – and all that time you were living all yours!'

The cops had gathered their thoughts now and command had passed without discussion to a short, stocky man with sergeant's stripes. At his signal, they moved in and seized the Doctor, Rose and Waller. None of them resisted.

A black-gloved hand closed over the lens of the

camera, blocking its view of the scene – and a moment later, it went dead.

But by then, of course, it was far too late.

It had been an amazing two months.

The Doctor's speech had calmed tensions on the streets. Many rioters had just quietly given up and gone home to think about all he'd said. The police had been able to deal with the rest.

Later that night, Cal Tyko had appeared on 8 News and talked nervously about micro-organisms that fed off brainwaves. He had been arrested immediately, of course – but his claims had been scrutinised by a score of doctors and they'd all concluded that he was telling the truth. Domnic himself had been examined many times over.

A serum had been synthesised within days. The doctors had said it would alter the composition of human brain fluid, just enough to make it unpalatable to these stealers of dreams. An hour later, it was revealed that the serum was actually coloured water and that the doctors had imagined its beneficial effects. But work had continued and distribution of a real cure had begun a fortnight later.

The take-up had been huge – although some people had stayed away, still scared of the idea of being able to visualise all they liked. Or perhaps of the opposite: of finding out the truth. Most of them had had their minds changed by the news media swinging its weight behind the vaccination campaign.

The Big White House hadn't been closed down yet, but most of its beds were empty. Domnic, Rose Tyler and Captain Jack had been among the first to be discharged. Kimmi Waller had been one of the last.

Her release had dominated the news last week. The Chief of Police, in a newspaper interview, had said there would be no charges over the theft of police equipment – and indeed that Waller would be welcome to join her force for real, if she cared to apply. Apparently, during her fictional career, she had made more arrests than almost any other officer.

The police had still been trying to work out what to do with 'Hal Gryden' – still trying to decide if he was hero or villain – when the decision was taken from their hands. He had disappeared from a locked room during the night and hadn't been seen since. Only Domnic knew where he had gone and he wasn't saying.

An election campaign was well under way, with hundreds of candidates all promising to deliver dreams if they were voted into office.

And a bunch of historians had revealed the name of their world, at last, having sifted through the evidence without delusion or preconception. Colony World 4378976.Delta-Four, it turned out, had once been known as Arkannis Major.

Which, everyone agreed, was a bit dull.

He had hurried through the jungle, not caring about a few scratches this time. Every so often he had thought he could hear voices ahead of him. He'd dismissed them as products of his imagination, before realising that they *were* real.

He had reached the blue cabinet just as its door shut with a final-sounding thud. He had run up to it but hadn't known what to do. Cry out? Knock on the door?

What would he have said if somebody had answered?

He had walked round the box, staring at it, agonising over his indecision.

He had completed his circuit and been surprised to find Rose Tyler in front of him.

'Hi.'

'Er, hi,' Domnic had stammered. 'I just… I didn't want to… I felt…'

'I know. Sorry 'bout sneaking off like that. The Doctor's not keen on goodbyes.' Domnic hadn't said anything, so Rose had continued, 'I think it's all the adoration – makes him a bit embarrassed.'

Captain Jack had popped his head out of the door. 'You ask me, he's missing out on the best bit. Why else put our necks on the line, if not for the adoration? Coming, Rose?'

'OK, yeah.'

Jack had glanced at Domnic. 'Listen, mate, the Doctor said you should try to re-establish contact with other human worlds, get them to send you all the fiction they have. He said you've got so much to look forward to: Hitchcock, Proust, Blyton, Dennis the Menace.' And then he'd disappeared again.

'No, really,' Rose had laughed, 'that's what he said: Dennis the Menace.'

Domnic had swallowed. 'Will I… Will we see you again?'

'Doubt it,' she had said regretfully. Then, turning back to the cabinet, she had paused and added, 'Well… maybe in your dreams.'

Then she'd darted forward, kissed Domnic quickly on the cheek and disappeared with a wink and a grin.

The door had shut again behind her and Domnic had been startled by the rasping, grating sound of some unearthly engine.

And he'd watched agog as, yet again, something unbelievable had happened.

The new show came on promptly at seven. It was about Hal Gryden, of course, travelling in his spaceship to other worlds and teaching them how to dream – and it was everything that had been promised of it.

Domnic Allen was glued to the screen, hardly daring to blink until the episode was over. He could almost feel new ideas expanding and combining inside his head.

That night, for once, he – like many others – would go to sleep happy.

And dream of monsters at the foot of the bed.

# About the Author

Steve Lyons has written nearly twenty novels, several audio dramas and many short stories, starring characters from the X-Men and Spider-Man to the Tomorrow People and Sapphire & Steel. He has also co-written a number of books about TV shows, including *Cunning: The Blackadder Programme Guide* and the bestselling *Red Dwarf Programme Guide*.

His previous Doctor Who work includes the novels *Conundrum*, *The Witch Hunters* and *The Crooked World*, audio dramas *The Fires of Vulcan* and *Colditz*, and work for the official *Doctor Who Magazine*. He lives in Salford, near Manchester.

# Acknowledgements

First off, thanks to Neil Harding for passing on an anecdote about an employer who thought that those taking part in role-playing games were 'detached from reality'. In typical *Doctor Who* fashion, I exaggerated this to form the basis of my book. Thanks also to Neil for technical assistance as usual, and to Helen Raynor at the *Doctor Who* production office for trusting me with a couple of Top Secret scripts so I could find out a bit more about this Captain Jack guy!

And of course this book wouldn't be what it is without my editor, Justin Richards. In fact, I'd like to take this opportunity to thank all those wonderful people who've let me play in the Doctor's universe for the past thirteen years – and in particular I'm hugely grateful to Peter Darvill-Evans for taking a chance on an untried writer all that time ago.